Kilraine!

Kilraine: the fast gun who left to protect his family; Grace Jefferson: Kilraine's wife who was shot when their ranch was raided by night riders; Lucy Jefferson: the daughter he's never seen; Sam Jefferson: Grace's father – they murdered him claiming self-defence; Carver Giles: he killed to have it all; Eli Carter: the brave young man who stood up for the town; Utah Williams: Giles' hired killer. . . .

A cast of characters larger than the West itself comes to life in a classic tale of good against evil, in which the final showdown would pit three guns against a living ghost and possibly tear a family apart forever.

Kilraine!

Jack Crow

A Black Horse Western

ROBERT HALE

© Jack Crow 2020
First published in Great Britain 2020

ISBN 978-0-7198-3073-0

The Crowood Press
The Stable Block
Crowood Lane
Ramsbury
Marlborough
Wiltshire SN8 2HR

www.bhwesterns.com

Robert Hale is an imprint
of The Crowood Press

Typeset by
Derek Doyle & Associates, Shaw Heath
Printed and bound in Great Britain by
4Bind Ltd, Stevenage, SG1 2XT

This one is for Sam and Jacob

CHAPTER 1

Having begun its life high up in the snow-capped mountains, the slight breeze flicked a long strand of black hair across the fine features of Grace Jefferson's face. Without thinking about it, she tucked it back behind her left ear and continued her chore of hanging out the washing on the long strands of wire that served as a clothes line. When the last item was hung, she dried her hands on her once-white apron and bent down to retrieve the old wicker basket from the short grass. Placing it on her hip, she turned to go back into the house but stopped and looked around at the surrounding landscape. The vista boasted lush meadows split by a narrow creek. Further back at the foothills were large stands of pine and yellow-leafed aspen, currently in their full autumn splendor. She loved this time of year, especially here in the valley when the color of the leaves as so varied and plentiful.

Grace was twenty-nine and had lived in the Serenity Valley since she was ten. Such a long time had passed since she was that skinny kid, having grown into a five-foot-nine, brown-eyed, raven-haired, determined woman.

A drab-gray dress covered her still thin frame and it looked out of place against the lush beauty of the high country.

Grace remembered what it had looked like when they'd first arrived. Her father had just returned from the war, resigned his commission, packed up his family, and moved west from Virginia.

With a hint of sadness, she remembered too that brutal first winter, which had devastated their family by taking her younger brother, Joshua, after contracting pneumonia. And how the locals had pitched in to help build their barn, and then her mother's death three years after that of her brother. Then, for the next nine years, it had just been Grace and her father, Sam, and occasionally, a ranch hand.

When Grace was twenty-two, a man had come into her life. To her, he was kind, caring, and honest, and treated her better than she'd ever known a man could. To the rest of Serenity Valley and the town of Bowen, he was a man of violence, one to be feared. Even Grace's father shared that opinion of him.

Jared Kilraine was a gunfighter tired of his violent past and doing his best to escape it. One which seemed to catch up to him no matter how hard he tried to evade it, tearing down any life he'd managed to build for himself.

Eventually, the general consensus of the town was proved right, even though he'd done his best to avoid it. A young gun looking to make a name for himself rode into Bowen after word had spread that Kilraine, the man with the lightning-fast hands, was there.

The undertaker had buried the kid two days later, and Kilraine had ridden out on the third. He'd left behind him a wife carrying their unborn child.

Oh, they had warned her not to marry him. But what did they know? Grace clenched her fists until her knuckles turned white. If only they could have been left alone.

'Mama, riders coming,' Lucy Jefferson said to her mother in a melodic voice. The child's approach had been so quiet that her mother had failed to notice her presence. Grace ran her free hand through the girl's mussed hair as Lucy pointed along the valley to where a group of riders was crossing the creek.

The bench on which the ranch house sat gave a full view along the valley, and anyone on approach could be seen from a fair distance.

Grace's heart skipped a beat as she noticed them splash through the water and up the near-side bank. She watched them for a while, knowing who they were but hoping she was mistaken. She wasn't. 'Lucy, run along and get your grandpa. Quickly now.'

Brown-eyed Lucy Jefferson, aged six, slim, and dark-haired, remained unmoving. 'Why? I want to see who it is.'

'Get your grandpa and go inside, now!' Grace snapped.

But Lucy would not be moved. 'I want to stay with you.'

Grace swung to face her daughter, her anger rising at the sight of Lucy, hands on hips, defiance etched on her face. Immediately the memory of Lucy's father flooded her mind. Damn the man for giving her that one irksome, frustrating trait.

'Go now, young lady,' Grace said, her voice elevated. 'Do as I say!'

Instantly Grace regretted shouting at her as she watched the little girl's lips start to quiver. Tears formed and spilled from the innocent eyes and Lucy turned and ran off to find her grandfather.

After having seen the best part of sixty years, Sam Jefferson had accomplished most of what he'd wanted to in his life. Now as the years crept by, life was all about his daughter and granddaughter. That they would have a good life after he was gone, was all that mattered.

Jefferson wasn't an overly big man and age was starting to stoop his wiry frame. His once black hair was now gray and matched his eyes. And even though his body was starting to fail him, the determination to provide all he could for his girls was stronger than ever.

'Grandpa! Grandpa!' Lucy came running around the corner of the house. Sam smiled at her. She reminded him of Grace at that age.

'What's the matter, baby girl?' he asked, his voice full of tender warmth.

'There's riders coming up the valley,' Lucy blurted out. 'Mama said for you to come quick.'

Jefferson's mind raced. There would be only one reason for the urgent message. He patted his grand-daughter on the head. 'Thank you, Lucy. You run along inside now.'

He watched and waited for the girl to enter the house, before hurrying around the building to where Grace was standing, the wicker laundry basket dropped on the grass at her feet. 'What is it?'

His daughter nodded in the direction of the riders who were now on the upslope towards the ranch yard. 'Kel Moore and some of Carver Giles' men.'

Sarcasm dripped from Jefferson's voice when he said, 'Now, what do you suppose they want?'

The riders rode into the ranch yard, easing their horses to a halt in front of Grace and her father. Their leader, Kelvin Moore, was dressed in range clothes and rode a bay horse.

Moore was thirty-seven and stood a shade over six feet. He was the foreman of the Lazy G ranch owned by a man named Carver Giles. The others were sup-posed to be ranch hands, but gun hand was a more appropriate description. Moore stepped down from the saddle.

'Ain't no one said you could climb down off your horse, Moore,' Jefferson growled.

Moore rested his right hand on the butt of his Colt and said, 'Ain't no one said I couldn't.'

'What do you want?'

11

Moore stretched out a few kinks and said, 'Mr Giles sent us here for a talk to see if you've come to your senses about his offer on your ranch.'

Jefferson snorted derisively, 'Well, I guess you just wasted your time then, Moore, because I already told your boss I ain't selling. To him or any other man who waves money under my nose.'

'Yes, sir. Mr Giles said that,' Moore allowed. He turned his attention to Grace. 'Ma'am, maybe you can talk some sense into your pa. Mr Giles, he means to have this land. One way or another.'

Grace's answer was terse, 'My father can speak for himself, Mr Moore. Does he look like he's not in control of his senses?'

Moore nodded and focused his attention back on Jefferson. 'Mr Giles made you a fair offer, Jefferson. But I'll tell you right now, it don't make no never mind whether you take it or not. In the end he will get your land, your grass, and your water. It's just up to you how that happens.'

A small fire started to burn deep inside Sam Jefferson. 'Get on your horse, Moore, and get the hell off my land!'

Grace placed a hand on her father's arm. 'Pa, ease up.'

'You'd best listen to her, old man. Would be a shame if something happened to her or that purty little girl of hers.'

The veiled threat was all it took for Jefferson to snap. 'Why, you son of a bitch,' he snarled and stepped forward, his hands curled into fists.

'Pa, stop!'

Grace's cry went unheeded as the old man's rage took control. Jefferson swung wildly and moved in close to the foreman. Moore dodged easily to the left and countered with a right that staggered Jefferson when it smashed into his jaw.

Moore smiled wickedly as he reached out and grasped the old man's shirt. He hit him three more times in the face, then followed up with a heavy blow to the stomach.

Grace launched herself at Moore, who pushed her away easily. She sprawled to the ground in an ungraceful heap. The foreman withdrew his hands, letting Jefferson fall, and stood over him. He spit in the dirt of the yard. 'Listen up, old man. Your time is fast running out. Mr Giles has been a patient man. So, you'd best make a decision, and soon.'

The four mounted men sat quietly smiling, their arrogance and confidence evident, and watched as Moore gave Jefferson a parting kick. He climbed back onto his horse and looked down at the old man, a scornful look on his face. After a mock salute, he turned his horse and they all rode from the yard, laughing and talking loudly.

Grace rushed to her father's side. 'Pa, Pa, are you OK?'

The old man groaned and opened his eyes. 'Stop fussing, girl. I hear you.'

His daughter breathed a sigh of relief. 'Can you move all right?'

Jefferson sat up with Grace's help.

13

'Oh, hell, Pa, you're bleeding.'

'You watch your cussing, girl. I'll be fine.'

'Pa, we need help.'

'No.'

'We need him.'

'I said no, Grace.'

'You heard him, Pa. What if next time he hurts Lucy?'

'I'm not going to ask for help from a hired gun,' Jefferson said with finality.

'He's not a hired gun anymore.'

The old man stared at his daughter. 'How do you. . . ?'

When he saw the look in Grace's eyes, he left the question unfinished. He'd not seen it since she was a little girl and he'd caught her doing something he'd disapprove of. 'Aw, hell.'

Deputy City Marshal Jared Kilraine knew that the cowhands were going to be trouble the moment they rode into Hobart, Nebraska, firing off their six-guns like there was no tomorrow. He shook his head, watching them drag their mounts to a halt outside of the Barn Door Saloon and scramble inside for their first drinks of many.

And it wasn't even dark. It was barely the middle of the afternoon in the middle of the week. So, what the hell were they doing in town?

Hennigan from Rafter H trying to assert his authority over the town again, Kilraine guessed. Sending his boys into town, have them kick up a fuss, and . . . yeah, there he was. Skull Crawford. Hennigan's hired gun. It looked as though today would be the day.

Kilraine drew back from the store-front awning post he'd been leaning against and headed for the town marshal's office on the other side of the street. He found his boss, Merv Gentry, sitting at his desk, having a late lunch. 'What's up, deputy?' Gentry asked around a mouthful of cold chicken.

'Looks like Hennigan is making his move, Merv. His boys just rode into town, and so did Crawford.'

'Is that what that noise was?' Gentry indicated with a toss of his head in the direction of the saloon.

'Yeah.'

Gentry studied Kilraine. His six-foot-two deputy had been with him for two years now. The man had ridden into Hobart one afternoon looking for a job. It just so happened that a vacancy for a deputy had opened due to the previous one's death. 'What do you want to do?'

'You're asking me?' Kilraine was a bit incredulous.

'I am. I'm not any good with a shooter. Not like Crawford.'

Kilraine took his dark hat from his head and ran a hand through his thick, black hair. 'They'll kick up a fuss to draw us down there. Which is why Crawford is here. He'll be meant to take care of me. I guess they figure without me, then you'll just roll over.'

Gentry shook his head in disgust. 'All for a puddle of water.'

'In this drought, water is like gold.'

15

Which was true. Without substantial rain soon, water would become scarcer than it already was. Hence the fight that was brewing over what remained in Randall Hilton's pond. Hilton didn't have beef or horses, but he had water. Water he wasn't using, and Hennigan wanted it. He aimed to take it and the only thing standing in his way was the law. Today was all about rectifying that matter.

'So, we wait and see what happens?' Gentry proposed.

'Something will. Sooner or later.'

'Can you take Crawford?'

Kilraine nodded. 'I can take him.'

CHAPTER 2

Things changed just before dusk, with the rattle of gunfire reverberating along the street. Kilraine put his cup of coffee on the battered desktop, picked up his hat and walked toward the door. Gentry, who'd been sitting in his chair, rose to his feet and crossed to the gunrack on the far wall.

The Hobart town marshal took down a sawn-off shotgun and broke it open. He reached into his trouser pocket and took out a couple of cartridges and fed them in. The barrels snapped closed and he joined Kilraine out on the boardwalk.

People were hurrying along the street, trying to get as far away from the shooting as they could. There seemed to be an atmosphere of expectation in the air. A round-faced man stopped in front of them on the street, and his expression spoke volumes. He looked scared and had a right to. It was his saloon they were wrecking.

17

'It's the Rafter H boys, Merv. They're just shooting up my place something fierce. Crawford is with them but he's just standing.' His eyes shifted to Kilraine. 'Waiting for you.'

The deputy nodded. 'You go back and tell him I'll meet him on the street in five minutes and we'll get it done. But tell him if his friends keep shooting up your place, I'll come down there and kill every one of them.'

'But there's five of them plus Crawford,' the saloon owner pointed out.

'Tip, I have six bullets in my gun. I think that'll be enough.'

Looking at the deputy like he was loco, he said, 'Oh. Sure.'

Shaking his head, the man hurried off toward the saloon and Gentry said, 'You figure he'll come out?'

'He won't be able to help himself,' Kilraine said. 'It's a matter of pride.'

'Do you ever get scared?'

The deputy looked at the town marshal. 'Once. Not anymore. I just accept the fact that I could die and that's it.'

Once, Kilraine had thought himself invincible, that his frame was actually ten-feet tall. But after a few years, he'd realized otherwise, and following that, he'd begun to wish that he'd never discovered his talent with a six-gun.

Eventually, he decided that he would like to settle down, have a life away from the gun. He'd met Grace and it had all seemed possible. There'd been a few hitches along the way, and they were preparing to have a family, looking forward to the birth of their first child, when his past had come back with a vengeance.

He thought of Lucy, wondering whether she had any of his features. Maybe his brown hair, or his brown eyes. Perhaps his stubborn streak. But he didn't know because Grace didn't mention it in her letters. She probably figured that it would be cruel to talk about Lucy when he was forced to stay away. Maybe one day. . . .

The gunfire in the saloon stopped and Gentry said, 'I guess this is it.'

Kilraine took his Colt from its holster and, out of habit, checked the loads. With that done he stepped down into the parched street and began his steady pace toward the saloon. Gentry did the same but crossed to the opposite side and walked steadily along the boardwalk, cradling the shotgun.

Up ahead the cowhands spilled from the saloon doors and out onto the street. Behind them, taking his own time, was Skull Crawford. The hands saw Kilraine and one of them said, 'There he is. The man who thinks he can kill us all. Is that right, big man?'

'If he don't, I will,' Gentry snapped from his position outside the saddlery.

They glanced in the town marshal's direction. 'You stay out of this, Gentry.'

'How many of you do you think I can get if I fire

both barrels at once?' he asked casually.

Uncertainty etched their faces as they contemplated the double charge tearing their flesh, pulping it into a bloody mass. Suddenly they didn't seem so confident, and their bravado began to wilt.

'Get off the street,' Crawford told them in a low voice. They looked at him briefly and then shuffled away.

'You sure you don't want our help?' one of them asked, eliciting a glare from the hired gun. One of his friends slapped him up the back of the head and said something about him being stupid.

Kilraine stopped no further that twenty feet from the lanky killer. 'Are we really going to do this all because of a puddle, Skull?'

Crawford shrugged. 'It's a mighty valuable puddle, Kilraine. Worth more than gold right now.'

The deputy studied him for a moment, having heard a lot about Crawford over the years, but most notable was the fact that the gunman only went up against another gun when it was certain he couldn't lose. Kilraine shook his head. 'It's about more than that. It's about money and power. Mostly power. Your boss is losing his grip on the valley now that the law is standing up to him. And he don't like it.'

'Maybe,' said Crawford.

'Where's the second shooter?'

The question surprised the gunfighter. Not that he let it show too much but the flicker at the corner of his left eye told Kilraine all he needed to know.

The time for talking was done.

Kilraine's hand flashed down and came up filled with a bucking Colt. The first slug hammered into Crawford's chest. The gunfighter hadn't even cleared leather. His hand released its grip on the butt and the weapon dropped back into the holster.

A second slug punched through the killer's throat, opening a bloody gash. Not waiting to see Crawford fall, Kilraine swung about and shifted his aim to the top of the hotel. Taking a step to his left at the same time that the shooter fired his rifle, Kilraine fired the Colt twice more, and the shooter cried out in pain. Dropping his weapon, which began to slide down the roof top, he toppled forward, and fell to the street with a sickening thump, his gun landing beside him in the dirt.

The deputy swung back to cover the hands, but Gentry already had them pinned down under the gaping barrels of his shotgun.

'I guess we're done,' the city marshal growled at them.

'Not quite,' Kilraine said. 'There's the matter of damages to the saloon.'

'We can't afford to pay that,' one of the hands blurted out.

'You won't have to. I'm going out to collect it from Hennigan.'

Gentry smiled. 'Good luck with that. The fool will probably try to kill you.'

Kilraine stared at the corpse of Crawford. 'That

would make it a doubly sad day for him then, wouldn't it?'

The big gray gelding snorted and pranced around when the deputy brought the animal to a halt so he could study the ranch yard before him. It all looked quiet. Maybe the rest of the hands were out working the range. Kilraine guessed he was about to find out. It was the morning following the gunfight and he figured that Hennigan knew by now that Crawford was dead, even though his hands were still locked up in the cells.

He eased the gelding forward, scanning the landscape cautiously before passing through the gate and into the ranch yard. Chickens were busy pecking and scratching at the dirt but upon seeing the man on the gray they scattered into the shadows of the barn.

The deputy climbed down and led his animal across to the trough, where it could drink. The water was low.

'Ain't no one said you could water your horse at my trough,' Hennigan growled as he pushed out through the screen door of the house.

Kilraine turned to see the man standing defiantly at the edge of his porch, Winchester in thorny hands. 'Just get the hell on that crowbait of yours and start riding back the way you came.'

'Can't do that, Lex. I've come out here to collect for damages your boys did in town.'

Hennigan spit into the dust of the yard. 'I ain't

giving you shit for what they done,' he growled.

'You ordered it done. You pay.'

'What about Crawford? He was with them. Collect it from him.'

'Can't collect from a dead man, Hennigan. So, I guess it's up to you.'

Hennigan's eyes narrowed. 'Crawford's dead?'

'Uh huh.'

The old rancher spit again. 'Knew the son of a bitch was all talk.'

'How about that money, Lex?' Kilraine asked.

'You go to hell!'

The Winchester bucked in the rancher's hands and the deputy felt the passage of the slug close by his face. Kilraine drew the Colt and snapped off his own shot. Hennigan staggered as the deputy heard the slap of the slug hammering into him. The rancher lurched forward like a Saturday night drunk lunging for his beer on the bar. He dropped the Winchester, which clattered to the hard-packed earth. Then he joined it, falling forward, face first. Hennigan died right there in the dirt, bringing to an end the trouble he'd been causing the valley.

'He dead?' Gentry asked.

'Yeah.'

'What did you do with him?'

'Left him out there for his hands to bury. Wasn't going to lug him back here and hurt my back doing it.'

Gentry nodded. 'Come into the office a moment.

There was a telegram came for you. It's in my desk.'

Kilraine followed him through the door and waited while the marshal got the message from his desk drawer. Gentry passed it over and the deputy unfolded it and began to read. It only took a moment or so to scan through it. Kilraine refolded it put it back in his pocket. 'It's from my wife.'

Gentry opened his mouth to speak, thought about it, snapped his gaping mouth closed before a fly flew into it, thought some more, and then said, 'You have a wife?'

'Yes.'

'Well, I'll be . . . why didn't you say?'

'Long story. I've got a little girl too. Name's Lucy.'

'What's she like?'

'I don't know, I ain't seen her.'

'Oh.'

'Mutual agreement. But now Grace wants to see me. There's been some trouble and they want my help.'

'What kind of trouble?' Gentry inquired.

Kilraine shrugged. 'She didn't say but it must be bad if she's asking me to come.'

'Are you going to go?'

The deputy stared at Gentry. The marshal nodded. 'Sorry, stupid question.'

'I'll leave in the morning after I sort a few things out.'

Gentry shook his head. 'No. Don't wait. Where do they live?'

'Serenity Valley in Montana. Town is called

Bowen. I'll ride over to Omaha and catch the train.'

Gentry nodded. 'Good. Get some supplies and put it on my bill at the store. Then get the hell out of Hobart. Go help your family, Jared. It sounds like they need you.'

CHAPTER 3

Grace placed the plates of stew on the table and watched as Lucy screwed up her nose at it. 'What's those things in it?'

'Vegetables,' Grace said, rolling her eyes.

Lucy's eyes glimmered defiantly in the low lamplight. 'I don't like it.'

'You haven't tried it.'

'I don't have to try it to know I don't like them. I don't like vegetables,' Lucy grumbled with a frown.

'You eat them, or you get nothing else, young lady. We go through this every night.'

'I don't mind.'

'Fine,' Grace snapped, collecting Lucy's plate from the table.

'OK, OK! I'll eat it,' yelled the little girl, grabbing for the plate before it disappeared and she went hungry.

Grace put the plate back down in front of her daughter and Lucy began to fork it into her mouth.

'I might go into town tomorrow,' Jefferson said to

his daughter, around a mouthful of food. 'There's a couple of things I need to get. Thought I might take Lucy with me.'

'Yes, please. Can I go, Ma?'

Grace looked at the excited expression on Lucy's face. She smiled and said, 'Why don't we all go?'

'Yippee!'

'I need to get some things from the store,' Grace told her father.

'Are you sure you're not waiting on something else?' he asked abruptly.

A hint of red came to Grace's face, but she kept eating and let the comment go. But Jefferson wasn't as obliging. 'How long's it been since you sent word?'

'Not long.'

'If he's got any sense he won't come.'

'Who won't come?' asked the inquisitive girl.

'Eat your dinner, Lucy,' Grace said.

The old man was about to say something else when he cocked his head, a puzzled expression on his face. 'You hear that?'

'What?' Grace asked.

'I thought I heard horses.'

Grace stopped eating and concentrated on listening. After a moment she realized she was holding her breath and let it out slowly.

'I don't hear nothing,' Lucy said.

'Anything. I don't hear anything,' her mother corrected.

The girl rolled her eyes at her mother's comment.

Jefferson said, 'I could have—'

Suddenly the window exploded inward in a shower of shattered glass as bullets smashed it into hundreds of razor-sharp shards, some of which raced the slugs across the room. Lucy screamed at the sudden ferocity of it all and Grace grabbed her roughly, forcing her beneath the table. 'Stay down, Lucy!'

'Mommy!'

Grace felt a blow in her back and grunted. Outside, the storm of gunshots seemed to crescendo before dying away and finally stopping. It was brief and violent.

Jefferson came to his feet and grabbed the Winchester, which had been leaning against the back-door jamb. He levered a round into the breech and fired through the shattered window into the dark at the retreating nightriders. Once, twice, three times. The final one was followed by a string of cuss words, which he chopped off when he remembered that Lucy was present.

He turned to make sure both girls were OK and saw Lucy hunched over her mother. The girl looked up at her grandfather, her tears glinting in the lamplight. 'She's dead, Grandpa. They shot Mommy.'

'Oh, Christ!' Jefferson exclaimed as he scrambled across to where his daughter lay. He checked her to see if she was still breathing. 'She's still alive, baby girl.'

He rolled Grace over to look where she'd been shot and found the bullet hole down low in her back. He needed to get her into town. 'Lucy, sweetie?'

'Yes, sir?'

'Take care of your mother while I go hitch up the team to the wagon. OK?'

'OK,' she said in a worried voice.

Taking his Winchester with him, Jefferson halted at the door and listened. He could make out the sound of retreating hoof-beats, so he slipped outside and hurried toward the corral.

Later he would swear that it was the quickest he'd ever hitched his team, and it wasn't long before the wagon rattled out of the yard with Grace and Lucy in the back.

Doctor Homer Jackson had just finished his supper when hammering on his door made him hurry toward it, thinking that it would crash to his hallway floor before he reached it.

'Hold on!' the middle-aged man shouted. 'I'm coming. Where's the blamed fire?'

He opened the door and found himself facing Sam Jefferson, his daughter Grace bleeding in his arms. Beside him was Lucy. 'They shot her, Homer. The bastards shot my Grace.'

Jackson stepped aside. 'Quick, bring her in, Sam. Take her through to the first room on the left.'

Jefferson pushed past the doctor and Lucy made to follow him. Jackson reached down and stopped her. 'In there is no place for you, young lady,' he said in a soft voice. 'Do you know where Widow Smith lives?'

29

Lucy nodded.

'Good. I need you to be a big girl now, Lucy, and go get her for me. Tell her it's important, OK?'

'OK.'

'Off you go.'

He watched her leave, and then turned to follow Jefferson into the other room.

Kilraine wasn't sure whether there were two men or three. He thought three. He'd never really gotten a clear look at them but was certain those back there were following him. Just days on the trail after getting off the train, all his old instincts had kicked in. Gone was the lawman. The gunfighter had returned.

He knew he should have killed them when their so-called leader had braced him in the last town he'd passed through after getting off the train. What was it called? Granger? More like Bastard. It was as rough as towns come, with no law to speak of. There was only a falling down drunk pinned to a star to help keep him upright.

The whores had no teeth and smelled of sweat. The saloon itself served snake-head whiskey and a lot of the townsfolk seemed to have the same last name. Granger.

Had Kilraine's horse not needed rest, he would have kept riding. Instead he'd left it at the livery, threatening the hostler that he'd nail his hide to the loose plank wall if anything happened to it.

The toothless, grime-covered man with a croaky

voice had assured him in no uncertain terms that the horse was as safe with him as the next feller's. Which did nothing to instill confidence in Kilraine. All it told him was that the next feller who rode into town stood just as much chance of losing his horse as he did.

As it turned out, the man was right and losing his horse wasn't the source of the trouble. It wasn't even the saloon. The trouble came from where it usually did for a man fast with a gun. He was recognized by one of the Grangers. One who considered himself to be the fastest gun west of St Louis.

Kilraine had tried to talk him out of it, but to no avail. Things really became interesting when Chuck Granger, the so-called fast-gun, called upon two brothers and a cousin to back his play. When the smoke had cleared, Chuck lay flat on his back in the mud of the main street, blood turning the brown water puddle he half lay in pink.

His two brothers and cousin hadn't even pulled their six-guns. When Kilraine offered for them to try, they declined and dragged the dead Chuck from the street, leaving twin furrows from his boot heels in the mud.

Until now. He was reasonably sure that that's who it was following him. He thought they might have given up after the first day, but it seemed they were a little more persistent than that. Probably building up the spine to get it done.

Easing his horse to a halt beside a narrow creek in the shadow of a high granite peak, Kilraine climbed

31

down and took a drink. The bank was eroded from previous floods and a tall tree had its roots exposed like a tangle of yarn. He turned and pretended to adjust the girth on his horse, all the while taking in his surroundings. This would do. He'd make camp here for the night. If they were going to come for him, then let it be on his terms.

The attempt to bushwhack him after dark was so clumsy and ill-conceived that Kilraine almost felt sorry for them. But when he thought about what they planned to do to him that feeling went away.

Their first mistake was riding their horses in too close to his camp. A deaf man could have heard them coming from a mile away. Then as they approached on foot, the loud whispers carried on the still-night air. The third and final mistake was not leaving a man in the dark outside the firelight. Instead they came in together, the glow of the fire illuminating them perfectly.

As Kilraine watched the taller of the three approach his bedroll stuffed with grass, he thumbed back the hammer of the Winchester tucked snugly against his shoulder. With a stupid grin, the man raised his unholstered six-gun and fired three times, each shot causing the blanket to jump.

Gun thunder rolled across the grassy meadow and echoed from the face of the nearby mountain. As it died away the man leaned forward and pulled back the blanket, wanting to inspect his handiwork.

He stumbled backwards as though someone had

thrown hot water into his face. The six-gun came up and his head swiveled left and right looking for Kilraine, his companions doing the same thing, shocked that they had allowed themselves to be deceived so easily. Even from where he was situated, Kilraine could see the open fear etched deep in the men's faces.

Then he squeezed the trigger.

The Winchester slammed back against Kilraine's shoulder as it discharged the .45-.70 slug with a roar. The first would-be killer jerked as it punched into his chest, forcing him to lurch back a step. He sat down hard, his mouth opening to draw breath into his shattered lungs.

Kilraine worked the lever, ejecting the spent casing, and rammed home a fresh one. He squeezed the trigger again and the second man fell just as the rifle in his hand fired. Repeating his motions, he dropped the third, who had turned to run, abandoning his friends to save himself. It was over in a matter of seconds. Cold, calculating, and a necessary evil.

When he re-entered the firelight, Kilraine checked on the first man he'd shot. The fellow was dead, so he moved on to the next. This one was dead also, however, when he got to the third man, he found the original Granger brother was still alive. When he rolled him over onto his back, he could see blood staining his lips and the trickle coming from the corner of his mouth. The killer moaned and opened his eyes. He stared at Kilraine and said with a voice thick with blood, 'You son of a bitch, you lured us into a trap.'

'You can't complain,' Kilraine told him stoically. 'You brought it upon yourself when you decided to come after me.'

'Go to hell.'

'Probably will. If I see you there, be ready. I'll kill you all over again.'

Then Granger uttered a muffled curse and died.

Coming to his feet, Kilraine shook his head. 'The worst thing about shooting bastards like you is having to bury your sorry asses afterwards. Shit.'

The sun had just appeared over the eastern horizon when Doc Jackson emerged from the procedure room where he'd been tending Grace. After being kicked out, Jefferson had haunted the hallway, pacing back and forth, not seeing the worn carpet hallway runner beneath his feet, awaiting news of his daughter's condition. He stepped forward and asked, 'How is she, Homer?'

With a grim expression on his face, the doctor spoke as he shook his head, 'I don't know, Sam. She's tough, I'll give her that, but the next day or so will tell the story. If she can get through that, then I'd say she has a fighting chance. We just have to wait and see.'

'Can I see her?'

'Not just yet, Sam.'

The old man nodded. 'I need to go back out to the ranch and take care of a few things.'

'Can't any of your hands look after them for you?'

Jefferson's expression changed. 'I don't have any. The last ones left two weeks ago after Giles started threatening them. It was more than they were willing to risk for a job.'

'I knew you'd been having problems, Sam, but I didn't think they were that bad.'

'Well you just got a first-hand look at how bad things really are,' Jefferson said, stabbing a finger at the room where his daughter lay.

'Have you asked anyone for help, Sam?'

'There is only one man who could help us with the trouble we have, Homer. Maybe if I'd listened to Grace, then she wouldn't be lying in there near dead. But I'm a stubborn old fool.'

'You mean Kilraine, Sam?'

His face twisted with bitterness. 'That's exactly who I damned well mean!'

As deep in thought as Jefferson was on the ride back to the ranch, he knew that something wasn't right. He hauled the livery horse to a halt and studied his home from the low rise. There were strange horses in the corral and smoke was wafting from the chimney. There was also a rifle-wielding man guarding the approach where the trail topped the bench.

Jefferson reached down to grab the Winchester from the saddle boot but stopped himself. If he rode in there with it drawn, and if shooting started, there was a good chance that he would be killed. And if he died and Grace didn't make it, then there would be no one to watch over Lucy. So he made the decision to be smart about it.

Easing the horse forward, he rode toward the ranch house, letting the horse pick its own way over the rutted trail. When it started up the rise, the sentry walked out to block his path. Jefferson brought his mount to a halt and the man said, 'Where do you think you're going?'

'I'm going home.'

The man shook his head. 'Nope. You don't live here anymore.'

The old man felt an ember of anger ignite within him. 'Since when?'

'Since last night.'

'Spence!'

The man turned around and Jefferson saw Moore standing out front of the ranch house.

'Yeah?'

'Let him come up.'

Spence stepped aside, allowing the old man to pass. Once inside the yard Jefferson stopped the horse again. 'What are you doing here, Moore?'

'This is now Giles land. Everything you see. Or it soon will be in a couple of hours.'

'Says who?' Jefferson growled.

'The bank, of course. Just as soon as Mister Giles buys out what's left of your mortgage.'

'He can't do that.'

'Yeah, he can. Then the money you owe the bank will be owed to him. And guess what? He'll want it paid straight away. Now, I'm guessing that you won't be able to do that. So, you see, it's all just a matter of time.'

Jefferson's ember quickly fanned into a strong flame, his anger fast becoming a conflagration. The only dampener that kept it in check was the thought of Lucy. Moore smiled coldly and then sneered, 'How's your daughter? I heard she stepped in front of a bullet last night.'

And with that one snide remark, Sam Jefferson's life was over.

The comment was like a door being opened, creating a back draft which blew out his rage. He grabbed for the Winchester, all logic gone up in flames. Moore casually drew his six-gun and shot the old man from the saddle. All fire extinguished.

CHAPTER 4

'. . . is my shepherd, I shall not want. . . .'

To get to the ranch, Kilraine had to ride through Bowen. As he passed the cemetery surrounded by tall pines, he could hear the monotonous intonation of the preacher's voice presiding over a graveside service. Looking across at the small gathering, he recognized a few faces from the past. Burns, the livery owner, Grant, from the dry goods store, and Bentley, the owner of the Circle B ranch. Without further thought, he continued into town along the main street. Those townsfolk who weren't at the funeral, stopped and stared at Kilraine as he rode along. One, a man named Miller, who was the barkeep at the Western Pines Saloon, waved and called out, 'Hey, Kilraine, the funeral's the other way.'

Dragging the horse to a halt in the middle of the thoroughfare, he turned in the saddle then pointed his horse in the man's direction. The horse stopped near a hitch rail and the rider asked, 'What's that about a funeral?'

Miller, a thinly built rail of a man, looked confused. 'You mean you don't know?'

'Know what?'

'About the shooting?'

Kilraine was growing impatient. 'Just tell me what the hell you're on about.'

'Old man Jefferson. His funeral. They're out at the cemetery burying him now. You just rode past them.'

A cold chill ran down the deputy marshal's spine. 'When did that happen?'

'Day before yesterday.'

Kilraine began to ease his horse back from the rail and when it started to turn, Miller said, 'If you didn't know about the old man then you won't know about Grace.'

The gunfighter stopped the horse, his gaze burning deep into the barkeep as he waited for what came next.

'They shot her too, the night before they killed the old man.'

Kilraine's voice took on a hard edge. 'Is she still alive?'

'Last I heard she was. She's over at the doctor's place.'

'What about my daughter, Lucy?'

'She's fine.'

The gunfighter couldn't help but let out a sigh of relief. Miller said, 'I sure am sorry about seeing you under these circumstances, Jared. It's not good.'

'Who's the doctor around here now?'

'Still Homer Jackson. Same place.'

Kilraine nodded. 'Thanks. I'll head over there now.'

'Don't you want to know who done it? Maybe find them, give them some payback?'

'There'll be time enough for that.'

As Kilraine rode away, a cowboy came from within the saloon. He said, 'Who was that feller?'

Miller said, 'That was Jared Kilraine.'

'The gunfighter?'

'Yeah. One and the same.'

Kilraine knocked on the white door of the tidy home and stepped back, looking around, waiting for someone to answer. He noticed the well-tended gardens and the wisteria vine growing along the verandah supports. The house looked like it had been painted recently and the glass window panes were spotlessly clean. The door opened and he looked toward the person who stood there. It wasn't who he was expecting. It was Elvira Smith. She'd aged some but he still knew who she was. The woman's eyes widened with surprise when they took in the figure on the doorstep, and after a couple of attempts to get her words out, she said, 'It's you. You're here.'

'Yes, ma'am, I'm looking for Doc Jackson.'

'He's not here at the moment. He's at the funeral.'

There was movement behind her, and a little girl's

head popped out around the woman's skirt. Recognition flared in his eyes for there was no mistaking who she was. She looked up at him and asked, 'Who are you?'

'I'm—'

'He's nobody, Lucy. Now go back inside,' Elvira said abruptly, cutting him off.

'He doesn't look like nobody,' Lucy said.

'Go back inside, now, Lucy!' The woman's tone brooked no defiance.

The little girl pulled a face and turned away in a huff. Once she'd disappeared, Kilraine said, 'I want to see Grace.'

'You can't.'

'She's still my wife, Elvira.'

'You haven't been her husband for a long time, Jared Kilraine,' Elvira snapped.

'Are you my father?' Lucy asked from behind Elvira. She'd obviously doubled back and heard his name.

Elvira's face became a mask of abject horror as she realized what had just happened. Kilraine smiled at the girl and nodded. 'That's right, Lucy, I'm your pa.'

She turned and ran away, leaving Kilraine shocked and affected by their meeting. There was a noise behind him, and the gunfighter turned to see Doc Jackson coming through the gate. The doctor stopped short when he saw Kilraine and said, 'Is that you, Kilraine?'

'Yeah, it's me.'

Jackson pushed past him and said, 'Come inside, son. Don't worry about the woman unless she bites you. But even then, I've got a needle for that. Besides, we need to talk.'

'How's my wife, Doc?'

Jackson stopped and turned. The man had aged significantly since their last encounter, and he gave a grim nod, his eyes steely, and said, 'It was touch and go for the first couple of days. But she'll live. Come inside and we'll talk some more.'

Using his hat, Kilraine quickly brushed at his pants, then followed the doc inside, along the hall and into a well-lit living area. Jackson offered him a seat and then moved to place his own hat on the stand in the corner. The gunfighter hesitantly took a seat on the very edge of a wide lounge, not wanting to make it dirty from his trail-dusty clothes, and had only been there for a few seconds when Lucy came and sat beside him, placing her small hand in his.

Surprised, Kilraine looked down at her and she gave him a tentative smile. He smiled back and then gave Jackson a questioning look. The doctor nodded and said, 'I guess she figures with her mother laid up and her grandpa dead, that you're the one who'll take care of her. Your arrival couldn't have come at a better time.'

'You'd better tell me what's going on, Homer. Start with Grace.'

Jackson nodded. 'There was shooting out at the ranch. The riders weren't seen but we all know who it was. Grace was hit by a stray bullet and Sam brought her in to me.'

'How long ago was that?'

Jackson told him and then said, 'Sam went back out to the ranch the following day. That was when he was shot. Apparently, it's been taken over.'

'Will Grace wake up?'

'In good time, I think. Her being like this is the body's way of healing itself. I think she might wake up over the next day or two. I think she'll be happy to see you.'

Relief flooded Kilraine's body and he glanced down at Lucy. This time she gave him a bigger smile and he patted her hand. 'You hear that? Your ma will be fine.'

She nodded. 'I know.'

He looked back up at Jackson. 'What's the sheriff doing about this?'

Jackson shrugged. 'Not much. Cal Winters isn't exactly what you would call law-abiding.'

Kilraine frowned. 'What happened to Clive Groves?'

'Up and died. Heart gave out on him.'

'Damn.'

Jackson nodded. 'It just happened. No sign of it at all. He just dropped dead on Main Street.'

'What about Winters? Who's he work for?'

'A man named Carver Giles,' Jackson replied.

Kilraine frowned. 'Never heard of him.'

'Came here a couple of years back and took over Tom Buckley's place. Renamed it the Lazy G.'

'Why did Buckley sell?'

'Don't know. One day he was there, and the next he was leaving. I do know that Giles moved onto the range the next day.'

Kilraine sat there thinking, putting things together in his mind. 'Has Giles been up to anything else since he got here?'

'He's been acquiring land at a rapid rate. Of the six ranches out in that part of the valley, he now owns five. Including Sam's ranch.'

'How is that possible?'

'Giles bought the mortgage from the bank. Called in the payment the day Sam was killed. After all, dead men can't pay. It was mighty interesting that his men had already moved onto the place before he was dead. It was one of his men who killed old Sam. Feller by the name of Kel Moore.'

'Him I've heard of,' Kilraine said. 'He's bad. Killed more than his share of men.'

'That's him,' Jackson allowed. 'He's Giles' foreman.'

Kilraine stood up and so did Lucy. He stared at the doctor and said, 'I'll be back. There're a few things I want to do. Where's a good place to stay? It's been a while since I was last here.'

'You could try the hotel. The rooms aren't big but they're clean.'

'Jake Clemmons still over there?'

Jackson nodded.

'Good, I'll go and put my horse up, then head on over there.'

Kilraine made to leave and Lucy started to follow

him. He stopped and stared down at her. 'Where do you think you're going, missy?'

'With you.'

He shook his head. 'Nope.'

'Yes,' she said, a defiant expression on her face. He'd seen that exact look somewhere before.

'Shit.'

Her eyes widened. 'You cussed, Mom says you ain't allowed to cuss. She said if she ever heard me do it, she would wash my mouth out with soap.'

The gunfighter turned red after being chastised by his pint-sized daughter. He glanced at Jackson, the old medic standing there with a broad smile on his face. Then he said to Lucy, 'I've got things to do, kid. I'll be back after.'

He turned to walk away and once more, Lucy started to follow. Again, he stopped and stared at the little girl. This time he saw something in her eyes that made him change his mind. Fear. The poor thing was scared.

Kilraine sighed. 'Come on, kid. You got no objection, Doc?'

Jackson said, shaking his head, 'No, no. I think it might do the both of you some good, getting to know each other. Just stay out of trouble.'

'Yeah. I ain't had much luck of that over the years.'

After Kilraine had put his horse up, he walked along the boardwalk until they reached the hotel. People stopped to stare at the man and the child as they carried on, the little girl holding onto his hand.

Once in the hotel, the owner recognized him immediately. Clemmons hadn't aged well. His face was deeply lined and his back was starting to hunch. He took one look at Kilraine and said, 'As I live and breathe, Jared Kilraine. You sure have picked a bad time to come back to Bowen.'

'So they tell me. You wouldn't have a room for a few nights, would you?'

'Sure. Just for you?' he asked, looking at Lucy.

'For the time being.'

Clemmons passed a key across to him and said, 'Room six. I'll put your name on the register for you.'

Kilraine paid the man and climbed the stairs. Once at the top he walked along the hallway until he found his room. It was small, clean, and well-furnished. Maybe too well, with the furniture crowding most of the space.

The gunfighter dropped his things onto the bed beside where Lucy had taken up position, watching him intently. 'Why are you here?'

Kilraine studied her for a moment and said, 'Your ma sent word for me.'

'Where have you been?'

'Here and there.'

'Doing what?'

'At the moment I'm a deputy city marshal.'

'Why did you leave us?'

'Why do you ask so many questions?'

'That's what Ma says.'

'She's a wise woman, your ma.'

Lucy held his gaze for a while before asking, 'She'll be OK, won't she?'

'You heard the doctor, didn't you? He said she'd be fine.'

She climbed off the bed and walked across to Kilraine. Without hesitation she wrapped her arms around him and for the first time the brave little girl showed her other side. He tentatively returned her hug and when he did, Lucy squeezed him that much harder.

She stepped back and looked up at him. Kilraine could see the tears in her eyes. 'I'm glad you're here, Pa.'

He smiled at her. 'Me too.'

'You won't leave, will you?'

It was at that moment Kilraine knew he was never going anywhere.

CHAPTER 5

'You have to wait out here, Lucy,' Kilraine told his daughter as they stood on the boardwalk outside of the jail.

'Why, Pa?'

Here we go again. 'Because I need to discuss some business with the sheriff.'

'I can come in while you do that,' she insisted.

'No. You stay out here,' he said firmly.

He waited until she sat down on the edge of the boardwalk before saying, 'Don't move. I expect you to be there when I come back out.'

'Yes, Pa.'

Pa. The word sounded strange. Nodding, Kilraine turned away and walked over to the door. He pushed it open and went inside.

Cal Winters was sitting behind his desk, a cup of coffee in his hands, when Kilraine walked through the door. He looked up from his seat and said, 'What can I do for you, stranger?'

'You can tell me what you're doing about my wife,' the gunfighter said.

A frown came to Winters' deeply tanned face. 'Who are you?'

'Jared Kilraine.'

Recognition of the name crossed Winters' face and he leaned forward, placing the mug of coffee on the scarred desktop. 'You the gunfighter?'

'Used to be.'

'What are you doing here?'

Ignoring the sheriff, he repeated his own question, 'What are you doing about my wife?'

'Who is your wife?'

'Grace Jefferson.'

The man paled slightly. 'I've been investigating it. Haven't come up with anything though.'

'What was the verdict on old Sam's death?'

'Self-defence,' Winters said, this time with more confidence.

'Uh huh. Plenty of witnesses to back that up too, I gather?'

'That's right.'

'What were the fellers doing on his ranch?'

'The ranch belonged to Mr Giles. He bought out the mortgage.'

'Not then he hadn't. I heard he hadn't bought it until after Sam was already dead.'

Winters shrugged. 'Not the way I was told it.'

'Did you investigate it?'

'Of course, I did. Who do you think you are, coming in here asking me questions?'

Kilraine said, 'I'm just trying to find out the truth.'

He looked around the room and for the first time, noticed the dust and dirt layered on every surface. If the man looked after his office like this, then he could imagine what sort of an investigator he was. Instead of asking him more questions, the gun-fighter turned around and headed for the door. He'd find out for himself.

'Hey, where are you going?' Winters called after him.

'To do your job.'

Once Kilraine was outside, he found Lucy still sitting where he'd left her. He smiled and looked up at the sun. It was about mid-afternoon and he still had a couple of hours before the bank closed. He said, 'Are you hungry, Lucy?'

'Not really.'

'Come on, I'll buy. Maybe you can tell me a little more about yourself.'

She thought about it for a moment and then said, 'Can I choose whatever I want?'

'Sure.'

'OK, then.'

Kilraine sat watching her eat and for some reason was fascinated by it. Maybe it was the fact that he still couldn't get his head around the fact that she was his daughter. His own flesh and blood.

Lucy ate boiled ham and fried potatoes and fol-lowed it with apple pie. The gunfighter said, 'You won't eat your supper.'

'Mrs Smith cooks vegetables and makes me eat

50

them. She's mean.'

'What about your ma? Does she make you eat vegetables?'

'Uh huh.'

'Does that make her mean?'

'No, but Mrs Smith is.'

He chuckled and said, 'Once you've finished there, I'll take you back to the doctor's while I go and see another man.'

'Why can't I come?'

'Not this time, Lucy. I'll come and see you again later. OK?'

But Lucy wasn't listening. She was watching two men who'd just entered the café. They wore range clothes, and both were wiry thin. Kilraine asked, 'Do you know them, Lucy?'

She nodded without taking her eyes off them.

'Who are they?'

'They work for Mr Giles. They were out at the ranch when the man Moore beat Grandpa.'

'Wait, your grandpa was beaten?'

'Yes. They were there when it happened.'

As the men came past the table one of them stopped and said, 'Well, if it isn't little Lucy. How's your grandpa doing?'

The pair laughed out loud as they walked off. Anger boiled within Kilraine as he saw the expression on his little girl's face. He stood up and alarm gripped her. 'Where are you going?'

The gunfighter reached out and took her small hand in his large one. 'I'll be right back, I promise.'

He walked up to the counter and stood just behind the two cowboys. An air of unease settled over the café as people stopped eating and watched the stranger. Kilraine stood there for a few more heartbeats until one of the men turned, sensing his presence. The cowboy frowned and elbowed his friend.

Now both were facing the gunfighter, and Kilraine could see the owner behind them, and the worried expression on his face. However, it was one of the cowboys who spoke, 'Something we can do for you, stranger?'

'You could apologize to the girl for being so mean.'

They both chuckled. One of them said to the other, 'You think this asshole is serious, Jimmy?'

'He looks serious, Ed. Maybe we should tell him who we are before he gets to being out of his depth.'

Ed nodded and said to Kilraine, 'We work for Mr Giles over at the Lazy G. Just in case you're new to town, people around here don't mess with folks from there. Not if they know what's good for them. Understand?'

Kilraine nodded and then said, 'Now would be good.'

Both cowboys looked confused. 'What?'

The owner paled, knowing what was about to happen. This stranger was going to get his ass handed to him on a plate.

In a soft voice, Kilraine said, 'Now would be a good time to apologize to the girl.'

'Son of a bitch but he's persistent,' Jimmy said. 'Well, I guess he was warned.'

His hand had only just started to move when Kilraine's left snaked out and clamped down, immobilizing it. With his right hand, Kilraine drew his own six-gun and brought it up and down in a blur of movement. The thud seemed to carry throughout the room when the barrel crashed into Jimmy's skull. He buckled at the knees instantly and his eyes rolled back in his head. He fell to the floor without a sound and the gunfighter shifted his gaze to Ed.

The cowhand's jaw dropped at the speed with which his friend had been dealt. He tried to move his hand toward his own gun, a display that was pitiful to watch. The Colt in Kilraine's hand came up in a back-handed swipe and connected with Ed's jaw. A heartbeat later he joined his friend on the floorboards, out cold.

Holstering his weapon, Kilraine reached into his pocket and took out some money. He then handed it to the café owner and said, 'Keep the change. I'm sorry for the inconvenience.'

Then he turned and walked back to his table. Lucy looked up at him, wide-eyed. 'Why did you do that, Pa?'

'He was rude. Come on, I'll take you back to Doc Jackson's place.'

As they passed through the front door, the two cowboys still hadn't moved.

After leaving his daughter with Jackson and Elvira,

Kilraine walked along the street to the Cattleman's Union Bank. He pushed open one of the double-doors and entered. There were a few customers inside, but he wouldn't have called it busy. Unlike some banks he'd been in, Kilraine found this one rather well-lit despite the dark furnishings.

He stood patiently near the window and waited for his turn to come. When the teller called out, 'next,' Kilraine walked up to the counter. The thin-faced man behind it looked at him curiously before saying, 'How can I help you, sir?'

'I want to see your boss.'

The man cleared his throat nervously and said, 'Mr Wells is busy at the moment, sir. You will have to make an appointment for tomorrow if you wish to see him.'

Kilraine looked across the counter to a desk situated near the back corner of the room. Seated there was a round-faced man wearing wire-framed spectacles. He was alone. 'He don't seem too busy to me.'

'Well you'd be wrong,' the clerk said abruptly. 'Like I said, come back tomorrow.'

'What did you say his name was?'

'Mr Wells. I—'

'Hey, Wells,' Kilraine called out. 'You got time to see a customer, or are you working on another scheme to sell a man's land out from under him?'

Wells lifted his head so quick it was a wonder it didn't separate from his shoulders. The shock on the manager's face was there for all to see, and behind him, the gunfighter heard a couple of customers

54

murmur in low tones.

The manager came to his feet and hurried across to the counter. His eyes blazed and he snapped, 'What is the meaning of your outburst, sir?'

'I want to talk to you.'

'I'm busy, you can make an appointment like everyone else, and come back tomorrow.'

Kilraine shook his head. 'I aim to talk to you now, Mr Wells. We can do it here for everyone to listen in, or at your desk, which may afford you a little more privacy. I don't mind, but you might.'

Wells studied the determined face and then lifted the gate for the gunfighter to walk through. 'All right, come on through.'

The gate was closed and both men walked back to the desk and sat down. Wells focused his disapproving gaze on the man before him and said, 'Well, what is it?'

'You sold Sam Jefferson's mortgage to a feller called Giles. Why?'

Immediately the man looked flustered. 'I don't have to explain my actions to you, Mister. . . ?'

'The name is Kilraine. Jared Kilraine. Sam Jefferson was my father-in-law. Now answer the question.'

The man paled at hearing the name. 'I . . . I had my reasons.'

'How about you tell me then, because the way I figure it, you had no right to do what you did.'

'Mr Jefferson had been shot and so had his daughter. It looked like she would not wake up – I still think she hasn't – so I sold the mortgage to Carver for what was outstanding to the bank. There was no way they could make the next payment, the old man being dead and his daughter all but.'

'When did he buy it from you?'

'He approached the bank with his offer the day Mr Jefferson was killed. About noon I think.'

'So why did he have his men out there that morning?'

'I don't know, you'll have to ask him.'

'How much was outstanding on the mortgage?'

'Two-hundred dollars. It was almost paid out.'

'Where are the papers kept?'

'Here at the bank, why?'

'Who signed them?'

'Pardon?'

'Who signed them over to Giles. Did Sam or Grace?'

'How could they? One of them is dead and the other isn't likely to wake up. We had some new ones drawn up.'

Kilraine's gaze grew flinty. 'Do you still have the originals?'

'Yes, of course.'

'Get them.'

'I beg your pardon?'

'Get the damned papers, Mr Wells. You over-stepped your duties by selling the ranch to Giles.'

'I have done no such thing,' Wells said indignantly.

'I'm willing to bet that it won't hold up in court,

Mr Wells. If they both were dead, then maybe. But Grace is still alive. The only way that ranch could have changed hands is with her signature. Provided she is the sole beneficiary to the place, which I'm betting she is. Now get the damned papers.'

Astounded and red-faced, Wells climbed from his chair and walked across to a filing cabinet. He returned a minute later with the papers for the Jefferson ranch. Kilraine reached into his pocket and took out a roll of notes. He peeled off two hundred dollars and dropped it on the polished desktop.

'There,' he said. 'The mortgage is now paid out.'

'But what about Mr Giles?'

'Give him his money back,' Kilraine said, rising to his feet. 'Just make sure he understands that his papers aren't worth wiping his ass on.'

Jackson looked down at the papers on his table, too stunned to speak. He opened his mouth and then let it snap back shut. Kilraine said, 'Well, Homer, can I leave them with you for the time being or not?'

Jackson tried again. This time he managed to get out, 'Ah, yes. I can do that. But how on earth did you get them?'

'I pointed out to Wells the error of his ways.'

'Wow. This isn't going to go down well with Carver Giles. What do you plan to do next?'

'I'm going out there tomorrow and ask whoever is there to leave.'

'And if they don't?'

'Then I'll make them.'

'I wish you luck, I surely do.'

'How's Grace doing?'

'She's still the same. Don't worry, there's no visible reason I can see why she won't wake up in a day or so. Hang in there, Jared.'

'I need her to be all right, Homer. I ain't cut out to be a pa all on my lonesome.'

'Why don't you let Lucy be the judge of that. From what I've seen, you're doing pretty darn good so far.'

'She's a good kid. Grace has done a great job with her.'

'Between her and Sam I'd have to agree,' Jackson allowed. 'But Sam wasn't her father. I think that now you're here it will be even better. But only if you stay. Are you going to stay?'

'I've thought about it. I want to but I guess that will depend on Grace.'

'If that woman didn't still love you, and you her, you wouldn't be here. Now, you take care of what you need to, and I'll take care of the rest.'

There was movement in the doorway and Elvira poked her head around the corner. 'Doctor, I think you had better see this.'

Jackson frowned and was about to climb free of his chair when Lucy burst in. She threw herself at Kilraine and cried out at the top of her voice, 'She's awake! Ma's awake!'

Grace gave Kilraine a weak smile as he held her hand. 'You came.'

He nodded. 'There was never any doubt.'

'You'll never guess what we've been up to, Ma,' Lucy interrupted. 'Pa bought me food, took me with him when he went to see the sheriff. To the bank—'

'All right, Lucy, your ma don't want to hear about what we've been doing. She needs her rest.'

'OK. But it's good to have Pa here now that Grandpa is gone.'

Alarm appeared on Grace's face and right at that time, Kilraine wished the earth would open and swallow him up. He turned to Lucy and Jackson and said, 'Doc, can you take Lucy out for a moment, please?'

Jackson steered a protesting child toward the door and the gunfighter turned back to his wife. Her eyes seemed sunken and her cheeks the same. Her hair was mussed but the look on her face already told him that she knew what he was about to say.

'I'm sorry, Gracie. Sam's dead.'

He spent the next ten minutes explaining everything as best he could. Then the next ten holding her close. Somewhere amongst it all, Lucy came back in and joined them.

'What are you going to do now, Jared?' Grace asked him in a soft voice.

'Tomorrow I'm going out to the ranch to move along whoever is there.'

Her troubled expression was followed by, 'No. Jared. Leave it. Let Giles have the ranch. It's cost us too much already. I don't want to lose you as well. Not now you've finally connected with Lucy.'

'He's not going to get away with it, Grace. I'm a sworn peace officer—'

'Not here, Jared,' Grace pointed out.

'It don't matter. I gave my word—'

'Damn you and your word!' Grace hissed.

Kilraine nodded. 'I'll let you get some rest.'

He turned away and walked toward the door. No sooner had he placed his hand on the knob to turn it when Grace said, 'Jared.'

Kilraine turned to face his wife. 'Yes, ma'am?'

'You be careful. You have a family now.'

He nodded. 'I've always had a family. I just wasn't allowed to be with them.'

CHAPTER 6

The ranch still looked the same. Even from a distance. Kilraine studied the place as he approached it in the early morning light. His wary gaze flicked left and right, scanning for threats. It looked relatively quiet and the only sign of life came from the lazy column of wood smoke lifting from the stone chimney, staining the otherwise blue sky above it.

As he rode into the yard, Kilraine was met by a man coming from the house. The man had a confident swagger when he walked, and the gunfighter knew he was going to be trouble.

'Who are you?' the man asked.

'Who are you?' Kilraine said, repeating the man's question.

'The name's Spence.'

Movement behind the cowboy drew the gunfighter's attention and two more men emerged. Each one was armed with a Winchester. Spence said, 'I didn't catch your name, stranger.'

'I didn't give it.'

'Then what are you doing out here on Mr Giles' land?'

'It ain't his land.'

Spence's eyes narrowed. 'What did you say?'

'I said the land don't belong to him. He acquired it illegally. The bank had no right in signing it over to him.'

'So, what are you doing here?'

Kilraine watched the two men behind Spence move apart. Once they'd cleared their line of fire, they stopped. Kilraine said, 'I'm here to ask you nicely to leave.'

The cowboy chuckled. 'You're crazy. We ain't going anywhere. But if you know what's good for you, you will. Just turn that bronc of yours around and start riding. Maybe a good idea not to stop until you're clear of the territory.'

Kilraine sighed and dropped his right hand so it sat on his thigh, just forward of his Colt. 'Spence, this is going to go one of two ways. Both end with you and your friends leaving.'

'You do realize that there are three of us, right?' Spence asked, wondering whether the man in front of him was simple.

'You do realize that I have six bullets?'

Not the answer the cowboy was expecting, and it troubled him. This stranger was either crazy or confident, but definitely not simple. 'Last chance.'

'I've had a lot of them in my life. Expect to have a lot more.'

Spence cursed and began bringing his Winchester

up to fire. However, Kilraine's superior gun speed put a stop to it when he drew and fired with the speed of a striking rattler.

The Colt roared and the cowboy staggered as the .45 caliber slug hammered into his chest. Red appeared on Spence's shirt in a small wet flower. Shock set in as he realized that Kilraine had shot him, and he buckled at the knees. The six-gun fired again, and Spence fell back, his legs tucked beneath him.

The gunfighter shifted his aim to cover the man on the left. It was the cowboy on the right, however, who decided to join the fight and Kilraine had to adjust his aim. The Colt crashed again, and the man yelped, dropping the Winchester and clutching at his wounded left arm.

'You fellers done?' Kilraine asked.

The third man nodded dumbly. 'You didn't have to shoot them.'

'Was them or me. Your friend should be thankful I didn't kill him. Now get them together and get the hell off this land. And don't come back. I may not be so forgiving next time around. Don't forget to tell your boss he's got two days to move any cows that are on our range.'

'Who the hell are you, stranger?'

'The name is Jared Kilraine.'

'Who the hell is Jared Kilraine?' the solidly built, well-dressed man in his late forties bellowed. 'And what the hell is he doing on my land, killing my damned men?'

Carver Giles' glare was so hot that it was a wonder that the walls of his study didn't spontaneously combust. His hand had just broken the news to him about the fracas over at the old Jefferson ranch, and he was ready to shoot someone. Moore was able to give more details to fill in the story's gap. 'I've heard of him. He's a fast gun. Dropped off the face of the earth a while back and no one heard much about him. Then he resurfaced playing deputy marshal in a place called Hobart.'

'But what is he doing here?' Giles hissed, his lined face reddening further.

Moore shrugged. 'Who knows? Maybe Jefferson hired him before he died. How about I ride into town and ask a few questions?'

'No. We'll all go,' Giles said, rising from the chair he was sitting in. 'I'm going to see Winters, have the son of a bitch charged for murder and see him hanged. Then we'll be free of him.'

The rancher saw the expression on Moore's face. 'What?' he asked.

'I ain't so sure it's going to be that simple. From what I've heard, before he disappeared, Kilraine was good. Really good.'

'That's what I have you for. You're supposedly good with a gun. If he's a bigger problem than expected, then you can take care of him.'

'What do you want done about the Jefferson place?'

'Have someone keep an eye on it.'

'You want we should burn it?'

'No. I want that house kept right where it is.'

'OK, I'll send one of the boys over there right now.'

'Send two. And tell them to stay out of sight.'

'Yes, sir.'

When Giles' buggy rattled into Bowen mid-afternoon it was surrounded by four riders: Moore, and three other hand-picked men, two of whom were Ed and Jimmy, still nursing their ailments from the day before. The townsfolk watched the procession travel by, certain that if Carver Giles was bringing that many men to town there was trouble afoot.

They stopped outside the jail and the rancher climbed down. He and Moore went inside while the others waited outside with the horses.

Winters came to his feet in a hurry, his face red from where he'd been napping behind his desk. 'Mr Giles. What can I do for you, sir?'

'Your job, damn it,' Giles growled. 'That's what I pay you for. So how about you damned well do it!'

Winters frowned. 'What do you mean?'

'For starters, yesterday, some new arrival in town beat up two of my men over in the café,' the rancher snapped. 'Then this morning a hired gun named Kilraine killed Spence and wounded Duff.'

Winters seemed shocked. 'He killed Spence?'

'Yes, damn it. And I want him arrested for murder.'

'I take it that there were witnesses?'

65

'I'll give you as many as you need.'

'I'll see what I can do.'

'Take Ed and Jimmy with you. They can be your deputies.'

Winters wanted to say no but what he said was, 'OK.'

'Good. Go and find him. I'll wait here for your return.'

CHAPTER 7

Winters didn't have to go far to find Kilraine. The gunfighter had been expecting such a visit and was waiting on a seat outside the Cow Horn Saloon.

After getting back from the ranch, he'd visited Grace and told her what had transpired. At first, she'd been angry with him for killing a man but quickly realized that if he hadn't, they would have killed him.

'I don't like it, Jared,' she said. 'You're only one man. Carver Giles has so many.'

'What did you expect was going to happen when I showed up, Grace? That Giles would just go away and leave you all alone? No. You knew what would happen and that's why you sent for me.'

His last words had been harsh and Kilraine immediately regretted the tone he'd used. But Grace said, 'That was different. Pa was still alive then. Now he's gone and you are all we have.'

Kilraine reached out and took her by the hand. He said, 'It'll get worse before it gets better. I've seen

67

men like Giles before. Give him a little and he'll take it all. And there'll be more dying.'

'You don't have to be one of them.'

'I don't plan to be.'

And they'd left it at that. Now, the gunfighter waited for the next event to unfold.

He saw Winters and the two cowhands from the day before, coming along the street. Both wore badges, which didn't bode well.

Winters saw him seated on the boardwalk and changed direction, the two recent recruits following his lead. All three stopped short of the boardwalk and the sheriff said, 'I'm here to arrest you, Kilraine.'

'What for?'

'Murder. You killed a man out on the old Jefferson ranch. Witnesses say you killed him cold.'

Kilraine's hand was resting on his Colt. He shook his head and said, 'What I did was move some trespassers off my wife's ranch. Giles' men were on it illegally. I have the papers to prove that she owns it.'

'That's horseshit,' Jimmy growled. 'Mr Giles owns it. He bought the mortgage from the bank.'

'He may have thought he did but there was nothing signed by my wife, who is the legal owner. The bank had no right to sell the ranch in the first place. So, when I shot those men today, it was in self-defence because they tried to shoot me. You can go back and tell Giles that.'

Ed shoved Winters forward. 'Arrest him, damn it. That's what we're here to do.'

'Just hold on a minute, damn you,' Winters snarled. 'Are you saying you can prove that the land belongs to your wife?'

'Yes. And the others were trespassing.'

'And you say it was self-defence?'

'That's right.'

'Are you willing to come in until we get this mess sorted out?'

'No.'

'Damn it!' Jimmy barked. 'If you won't arrest the son of a bitch then I will.'

'Don't!' Kilraine barked, but it was too late.

The new deputy made to draw his six-gun. The gunfighter drew his own and then hesitated until Jimmy had his clear. The Colt in Kilraine's hand fired and the six-gun leaped from the new deputy's hand. He grabbed at it as a burning pain tore up his arm.

'Keep a tight rein on your deputies, Winters,' Kilraine snarled.

'You're mighty free with that Colt of yours, Kilraine.'

'Only if someone is trying to kill me.'

Winters shook his head. 'All right, you two galoots, get gone back to the jail.'

The sheriff turned away to leave but before he had gone too far, the gunfighter said, 'Tell Giles that if he keeps sending his men after me, he'll need to buy himself a good shovel.'

'I'll do that.'

*

'Give me your damned badge,' Giles snarled.

'What?' asked Winters.

'You heard me. You're done as a lawman in this town.'

'You can't do that,' Winters blurted out.

'I gave you the job, and I sure as shit can take it away.'

The sheriff was stunned. His jaw sagged as he tried to think of something else to say.

'Now!' Giles snapped, holding out his hand.

With a trembling hand, Winters reached up and unpinned the star on his chest. He handed it to the rancher and Giles said, 'Now get the hell out of here.'

Winters walked toward the doorway, hesitated for a moment, and then left. Moore stared at his red-faced boss and asked, 'What do you plan on doing about law now?'

'Who needs law? The only law around here is mine. Get a couple of the men together and take care of Kilraine tonight. I don't care how or where. Just do it.'

Later that night after he'd finished visiting with Grace and Lucy, Kilraine headed over to the saloon to have a drink and maybe a hand or two of poker. He never got as far as the bar. On seeing Winters hunched over a bottle in the corner of the room, the gunfighter changed direction and walked toward the man's table.

Winters watched him through angry eyes. When

Kilraine stopped, the one-time sheriff said, 'What do you want?'

'I heard you weren't sheriff anymore. Is that true?'

'What's it to you?' Winters snapped.

'A town without law is a bad thing. I've seen a few. Not pretty at all.'

'What the hell do you want me to do about it?'

The gunfighter shrugged. 'Just saying.'

'Well say it somewhere else.'

'What do you figure he's going to do?'

'Giles?'

Kilraine nodded. 'Yeah.'

'Come after you. He wants that land back.'

'What's he want it for, anyway?' the gunfighter asked.

'Greed. To be the biggest bull in this neck of the woods. Take your pick.'

Kilraine pulled out a chair and sat down. 'And you're just going to let him run you off?'

'I'm only one man.'

Silence descended over their table. At one of the others, Kilraine heard the high-pitched voice of a whore as she became excited for some reason. He sat and studied the ex-lawman's face and then nodded. 'I know you from somewhere. I couldn't see it before because of the name. But your name ain't Winters, is it?'

Winters stared at him, then his expression changed. He shook his head and said in a solemn voice, 'Winters is a name I've lived under for the past six or seven years. I used to go by Concho Briggs.'

'That's it,' Kilraine acknowledged. 'Came up out of Texas with one of the last big trail herds. Fast with a gun. Some say one of the best, and yet here you are under a different name.'

'You left out the bit where I was a drunk and couldn't find my way out of a whiskey bottle. But shooting a kid will do that to a man.'

'A kid?'

'Yeah. Grissom Kansas. I've been trying to piece together for years what happened. I was in a gunfight with Ted Bell. We were at it in the middle of the main street. I fired two shots. Ted fired one. He died from the first shot. His flew wide of me. The thing was, when the first bullet hit, he twisted some and my second missed. It hit the steel rim of a wagon wheel and ricocheted off it. You know how people get when they think there is going to be something exciting to see?'

Kilraine nodded.

'Yeah. Well they was lining the street, trying to see it all in its macabre glory. That ricochet could have went anywhere. Instead that hunk of lead hit some poor kid in the throat and cut one of them main blood vessels there. He bled out in his pa's arms.'

'That ain't your fault. Blame the kid's father for having him there.'

Winters stared at him with haunted eyes. 'He still comes to me of a night, you know.'

'I guess we all have our demons.'

'The thing is, I ain't never shot a man since. I still wear my gun but it's like a millstone around my

72

neck. A constant reminder about what I did.'

Kilraine noticed Winters' gaze shift toward the doors. He turned his head and through the blue smoke haze saw three men just inside the room. 'Who are they?' he asked Winters.

'The feller in the center is Kel Moore, Giles' foreman. The other two are Mills and Best. All three are handy with a six-gun.'

'I guess it's started then.'

'Looks that way.'

They watched the three men move to the bar and order a bottle. Each took one drink and then stoppered it, turning away from the counter. 'This is it,' Winters said.

'I think so,' Kilraine said, dropping his hand to his Colt.

The three men weaved their way between the tables until they reached their destination. Moore stared at Winters and said, 'You ain't needed here, Cal. Get lost.'

Kilraine waited to see what would happen. To see whether Winters had any semblance of pride left inside himself. It seemed he did, and he let Moore know about it. 'I'm good right here.'

The Lazy G foreman glared at him. 'You don't want to get mixed up in this, Cal. I'm warning you now. If you stay, you'll get the same as this feller.'

The gunfighter became aware that everyone in the saloon had stopped what they were doing and were concentrating on the unfolding events. He also knew that there was no way Winters would fire his gun inside the establishment. He'd be too aware of a wayward bullet finding the wrong target.

Kilraine came slowly to his feet. 'How about we take this outside where it's less likely someone will catch a stray bullet?'

Moore said, 'We could do that. But we won't.'

'Let me ask you a question, Moore. Has Giles got that many men he can afford to keep losing them?'

The foreman gave him a wicked smile, exposing crooked yellow teeth. 'You sound mighty confident.'

'Why wouldn't I be? I've got Concho Briggs backing me.'

The name had the desired effect, which gave all three men reason to pause. Kilraine's Colt came free of leather and the hammer went back. Stunned by the speed with which it appeared, neither of the Lazy G men had time to react.

The gunfighter waved it at Moore's two henchmen. 'You fellers step aside over there near that other table.'

He waited for them to do so and then said, 'Right, all of you unbuckle your gun-belts and let them fall to the floor.'

As they did this, an excited murmur rippled through the onlookers. The gunfighter glanced at Winters. 'You got those two?'

The ex-lawman raised his weapon above the table. 'Yeah. I've got them.'

'You'll pay for sticking your nose into this, Winters,' Moore rumbled.

The foreman was still glaring at Winters when

Kilraine housed his Colt and then hit him. Moore staggered back and plowed through a vacant table and chairs, scattering them. Kilraine followed, fists cocked and ready to continue the fight. He hit the foreman again, a stunning blow that rocked him to his boots.

The gunfighter threw another punch and it was only instinct that helped Moore evade it. He swayed to the left and the blow skidded across his shoulder past his ear. Then the foreman stepped in close and slipped a solid blow to Kilraine's ribs.

Air rushed from the gunfighter's lungs. He stepped back and Moore followed him. Another big swinging right fist would have put Kilraine down if he hadn't been aware it was coming. He ducked under it and then came up, his bunched right fist driving upward from down near his boots.

The human battering ram slammed into Moore's chin. It almost physically picked him up, but instead, the foreman's head snapped back, and he crashed atop a table. With a splintering crash it gave way under his weight and a once-functional piece of furniture was transformed instantly into matchwood, with pieces blowing in all directions.

Kilraine lurched forward and grabbed a handful of greasy hair, dragging Moore to his feet. He held the foreman steady and hit him again. Blood flowed freely from the foreman's mouth and the gunfighter was about to hit him again when Moore's head snapped forward aiming to deal a crippling blow to Kilraine's nose.

But the gunfighter saw it coming and dropped his head, tucking his chin into his chest. His forehead bore the impact of the attacker's stunning blow, but had it found its original target, the result could have been much worse.

The effect was reasonably profound and Kilraine let go of Moore, reeling back away from him.

The foreman did the same and backed off, allowing time for his head to clear. He gave it a shake and blinked the haze from his eyes. He directed his gaze at Kilraine and with a loud roar, flung himself at the gunfighter.

The two men crashed together but the impact of the foreman carried the gunfighter back with a momentum that caused them both to crash into the saloon wall. Kilraine grunted, raising clasped hands above his head, and brought them down in a savage blow to the back of Moore's neck.

The foreman stiffened and the gunfighter repeated the action. This time Moore dropped to one knee. As soon as it hit the floor, Kilraine brought his own up and hammered it into the foreman's chin, driving the man's teeth together with an audible click, remarkable that none of them broke considering the force of the blow.

Moore's eyes glazed and rolled back into his head as everything went black and he fell into unconsciousness.

Sucking in deep breaths, Kilraine stepped forward, blood evident in several places on his face. He spit on the floor and looked around the room.

The onlookers seemed to be stunned into silence at what they'd just witnessed. He stared at Winters. The man smiled. 'Ain't no one ever done that before.'

'There's always a first time,' the gunfighter panted.

'There is that.'

Kilraine turned his attention to Mills and Best. 'Get your boss out of here.'

They made to move for their weapons until the gunfighter stopped them. 'Nope. Leave them there.'

Both men glared at him before they picked up Moore and dragged him toward the doors.

Winters said, 'You know Giles ain't going to take this lying down, don't you?'

'I wouldn't expect him to.'

CHAPTER 8

'There's just no two ways about it,' Giles said rather calmly. 'I need to bring in a professional. Someone good enough to do the job.'

Moore sat on a chair in Giles' study, nursing more than a bruised pride. He said through puffy lips, 'It would have been fine if Winters hadn't interfered.'

The rancher nodded. 'It would seem that Winters has outlived his usefulness. Can I trust you to take care of him?'

'With pleasure.'

'No mucking around this time. Just damned well shoot him and be done with it.'

'Fine with me,' Moore growled.

Giles leaned forward in his chair and found a piece of paper to write on. He scribbled on it and said, 'I want you to send one of the men over to Croydon and have them give this note to Utah Williams. If anyone can get the job done it will be him.'

The rancher finished and waited as Moore rose

stiffly from the chair and walked over to the desk. The foreman took the message and said, 'I'll have Mills take it.'

'Good, see that it's done. And as for Winters, I'll pay you a hundred dollars to see that he doesn't bother us anymore.'

'Keep your money,' Moore growled. 'That's one I'm happy to do for free.'

'Are you really going to stay?' Lucy asked Kilraine. 'You're not just saying that?'

The gunfighter glanced at Grace who smiled at him, waiting for him to commit to an answer. He looked back to his daughter and said, 'I'm not just saying it, Lucy. I'm going to stay.'

'Are you going to live at the ranch with us?'

Again, another glance at his wife who nodded her assent. Kilraine said, 'I guess I am.'

'Yippee,' Lucy called out. 'We'll have so much fun.'

'I'm sure we will.'

The three of them were sitting on a bench seat outside in the sun. Doc Jackson had decided that what Grace needed on this fine day was sun to help her with her strength. So, here they were.

Suddenly, Lucy gave the gunfighter a puzzled look. 'How did you get that mark on your face?'

Kilraine rubbed at the bruise and said, 'I'm not sure.'

'It looks like a bruise.'

The gunfighter started to squirm on the seat at

being interrogated by his daughter. He looked to Grace for help, who saw the anxiety in his eyes and said, 'Why don't you run along and play, Lucy, so I can talk to your pa.'

'Aww.'

'Go, young lady. There'll be more time later to pester him with all of your questions.'

'Well, OK then. Can I talk to you later, Pa?' she pouted.

Kilraine couldn't help but chuckle at her. 'Sure, I'll look forward to it.'

He watched her go and then turned to face his wife. Her expression had already changed, and he knew there was no dodging the conversation to come. 'What happened to your face?'

'It's nothing.'

'Tell me the truth, Jared. If you want to stay and make a life with Lucy and me, then you need to be honest.'

He sighed. 'I had a fight with Moore, Giles' foreman.'

'Oh, Jared.'

'It's OK. They came looking for trouble and—'

'They?'

'Yeah, him and two others.'

'You didn't shoot them, did you?'

'No, no. The last I saw of them they were taking Moore out of the saloon.'

'All this will do is make things worse. I knew this would happen.'

'Grace, we've already discussed this. We both

know Giles won't stop until he gets what he wants. He sent those men after me.'

'So, what will he do next?' Grace snapped. 'Send a hired gun. Someone who can finish the job?'

Kilraine remained silent.

'Oh, God. You think he will, don't you?' Grace asked her husband, bewildered.

The gunfighter nodded. 'I think that it's a fair assumption.'

She came to her feet, all sign of being wounded gone with the wave of anger. She rounded on him and said, 'What about Lucy? What if something happens to her? You should never have come back. I was a fool for asking you to help.'

Her words had the desired effect and cut deep. Kilraine nodded and said, 'You're right. I'll leave in the morning.'

'Don't you dare! Lucy would be devastated.'

Exasperated, the gunfighter said, 'Well, what do you want, Grace? You can't have it both ways.'

'*I* don't want you to go,' Grace told him, contrite that her words had elicited such a response, and the prospect of losing him so soon after he'd come back to them.

'How many ranches has Giles taken over since he's been here?'

'Four before he took ours.'

'And what happened to their owners?'

Grace thought before answering. 'Olsen of the Broken O sold up and left overnight. Hennigan of the Crooked H died after he fell from his horse. Jed

81

Cramer of the Double C was killed by rustlers, and. . . .'

Her voice trailed away.

'And?' prodded Kilraine.

'Byron Mulligan from the BM Connected died after he was shot by persons unknown.'

'And each time, Giles stepped in and took over the land, didn't he?'

'Yes.'

'Now he's tried it with your ranch.'

'Yes.'

'He will keep going until he has it all. The whole of the valley. And now that there is no law. . . .'

'What do you mean there's no law?' Grace asked, cutting him off.

'Giles took Winters' star away.'

'You could do it,' Grace blurted out.

'Whoa, Grace. One minute you don't want me butting in, and then you tell me to pin the star on. Is that it?'

'Yes, no, maybe. Oh, I don't know.' She clenched her fists at her confused frustration.

'I do. I'm not putting on the badge. I'll send word back to Gentry and tell him I'm staying. I'll help out with the ranch and deal with the trouble if it comes looking for me. But I'll not go courting it if it's going to put you and Lucy in danger.'

'I want you to do more than help out on the ranch, Jared.'

'What do you mean?' he asked, unsure of where this was going, refusing to hope for more.

'I want you to live there with us. I want us to be a family. I want you, damn it. I still love you and I want you back.'

The words stunned Kilraine, so much so, that he couldn't speak. Instead, he kissed her, and she kissed him back.

Utah Williams threw in what he thought might've been a winning hand had the pot not climbed to unexpected heights. Three aces he held, but for some reason the dandy opposite him just seemed to want it more. In the end he tossed it in the guts.

The dandy began raking the chips toward himself with a broad grin on his face. Williams stared at him and said, 'Just hold up a minute.'

The entire Bulldog Saloon seemed to sense trouble, and amongst the noise that reverberated around the room, it seemed nigh impossible that they would all hear his words. But they did as the whole room went quiet.

Williams' cold blue-eyed gaze caused the man to freeze. His name was Olsen and he'd arrived on the morning stage. His eyebrows knitted and he asked, 'What's the problem?'

'I believe we have a problem,' Williams said, matter-of-factly.

'A problem?' Olsen said nervously. 'Why would we have a problem?'

'For starters, I don't mind losing at cards. Matter of fact, I'm not that good at it so I lose more often than I win. But it still don't stop me playing.

83

However, I do have a problem with losing when the feller I'm losing to is a cheat.'

An audible gasp went around the room. Cheating was bad. But cheating Utah Williams was a whole lot worse. Olsen grew nervous and then gathered himself as he tried to deny what he was doing, filling his voice with as much indignation as he could. 'Where I come from, sir, we shoot people for less than that.'

'Can you prove you weren't?'

'I don't have to.'

'Yeah, you do. Now take your hands off those chips before I take a handful and ram them down your throat.'

Olsen paled and drew his hands back as though the poker chips had just scalded his flesh. He flicked his hand and a Derringer appeared as though by magic. However, he never came close to squeezing the trigger. Instead, the tabletop erupted as a .45 caliber slug smashed through it, spraying knife-edged splinters and poker chips into the air.

The misshapen slug punched into the gambler's chest, tearing at flesh. The blow caused him to lurch back then over balance. The gambler crashed to the floor, chips landing all around him.

Williams came to his feet from his chair, a smoking Colt in his right hand. The others at the table had skittered their chairs back and retreated well out of the way at the first sign of weapons. The gunfighter walked around the table and stared down at Olsen. The man's mouth opened and closed like a fish out of water as he tried to draw breath into his ruined lungs.

Blood ran from the corner of his mouth and a gurgling sound came from the back of his throat. Williams leaned down and reached into the gambler's left sleeve. When he stood back up, he held three cards in his hand. All aces.

'Would you look at that,' a bystander gasped. 'He was cheating after all.'

The light in Olsen's eyes faded and he died. Williams tossed the cards to the floor, one landing in the middle of the dead man's chest. He turned away and casually walked up to the bar, where he ordered a drink. He'd give it two minutes before the sheriff arrived and another one before he was ordering him out of town.

But before the sheriff could arrive, another man came through the doors to see him. Stepping in beside him at the bar, the stranger said, 'Utah Williams, I have a message for you.'

The gunfighter turned and studied the cowboy next to him. 'What message?'

Mills reached into his top pocket and using two fingers took the folded piece of paper out. He passed it across to Williams, who quickly perused it. The message was from a man named Giles and he was offering him a thousand dollars to kill a man, which the writer had conveniently forgotten to name. Not that it mattered for Williams. He would do the job anyway. Especially for a thousand dollars.

Williams looked up from the piece of paper and

stared at Mills. 'I'll be ready to go in the morning.'

The doors of the saloon swung open and the sheriff walked in, a scowl on his face. Williams took one look at the expression and said, 'Maybe a little sooner.'

CHAPTER 9

Winters was nervous as he walked along the darkened boardwalk. The heels on his boots made a loud clunking sound each time they contacted the hardwood boards. He was headed back to his room after another night of carousing with his non-existent friends. Not that he cared, he was quite happy with his own company.

He stepped down from the boardwalk and crossed over the intersection of Main and First. Then up onto the boardwalk on the other side. Winters continued to make his way past the saddlery, bank, and the dry goods store. He reached Second and had only just stepped down onto the street when a six-gun barked in the darkness.

A slug hammered into his side, knocking the air from his lungs. Winters staggered and fought to stay erect. He clawed at the Colt on his hip, trying to free it so he could shoot. But the bushwhacker fired again and this time the bullet burned deep.

Winters went down on one knee as his strength began ebbing away rapidly. His thoughts were still for his Colt and he tried relentlessly to free it from its holster. He felt blood start to well in his throat and his breathing became more difficult.

A dark shape loomed over him and Winters used some of his last remaining strength to look up. 'You . . . son of a bitch.'

The six-gun crashed a final time and Winters fell face down in the dirt.

Kilraine was sitting outside enjoying the evening with Grace when he heard the shots. He sat forward and listened, waiting for another to filter out of the night. 'That was three,' Grace said nervously. 'I wonder what happened.'

The gunfighter came to his feet and dropped his right hand down to the butt of the Peacemaker. 'Go inside, Grace. I'm going to take a look.'

'Be careful, Jared,' she told him.

'I'll be fine.'

He hurried through the gate and out onto the street. As he made his way along the rutted surface, he could see people starting to gather, calling to each other. Closer now, Kilraine heard a voice say, 'He's been shot.'

Another said, 'Who is it?'

'Winters.'

A third voice, 'Couldn't have happened to a nicer feller.'

Kilraine pushed amongst the gathering crowd

and as he broke through took in the scene before him. Winters was on the ground with a man hunched over him. 'Move back,' the gunfighter snapped. 'You're all blocking out the light.'

'Who the hell are you?' a man snapped. Then, 'Oh, it's you, Kilraine.'

A murmur ran through those present as the gunfighter crouched down beside the fallen man.

'He's still alive,' the townsperson who'd been checking Winters said. 'Not for much longer, I'd wager though.'

Kilraine lifted his gaze and growled, 'Not if you do nothing. Get Doc Jackson.'

The man lurched to his feet, stung by the sharp words. He pushed through the crowd and disappeared. Kilraine said, 'Concho, you hear me?'

'Who's Concho?' a voice from the crowd asked.

The gunfighter cursed softly. 'Winters, can you hear me?'

A moan escaped the man's lips.

'Winters, who did this to you?'

Another moan came out as he tried to speak.

'Come on, you can do it. Who shot you?'

'Mo—'

'Who?'

'Mo – Moore.'

'Did he say Moore?' a man asked Kilraine.

'I think he did,' said another.

'Why would Kel Moore shoot him?'

'Why wouldn't he?'

'All right,' Kilraine snapped. 'Knock it off. If you

don't need to be here, how about you go away.'

The crowd grew hushed at the gunfighter's words. He stayed with Winters until Jackson arrived and then helped with the wounded man's transportation back to Jackson's surgery. When Kilraine left the room, he found Grace waiting for him. 'What happened, Jared?'

'He was shot by Moore.'

'Kel Moore?' she asked. 'But why would he do that?'

'Falling out amongst thieves. It looks like he bushwhacked him before he even knew he was there.'

'Oh, Jared, what's happening to this town?'

'Lawlessness.'

She saw the expression on his face and her eyes widened with realization. 'You're going after him, aren't you?'

'Just as soon as the sun comes up.'

'Be careful, Jared.'

'I intend to.'

Kilraine's first stop the following morning was the sheriff's office. He tried the door and found it open. When he entered, he found a young man with blond hair sitting behind the desk, then he noticed the badge.

The kid looked surprised to see the gunfighter and when Kilraine asked him who he was, the young man announced proudly, 'I'm Eli Carter. The new sheriff.'

'The hell you are,' Kilraine said. 'What fool put a

kid into this office?'

Carter looked offended. But if the kid wanted to live to see his next birthday, this wasn't the job for him. Not now. Kilraine pressed him. 'Well? Who?'

'Ah . . . the mayor,' he stammered.

'Hannigan? Why did he pick you?'

'To go after Moore for the murder of Winters.'

The gunfighter shook his head. 'Of all the fool things.'

'What?' Carter asked.

Kilraine walked across to the gun rack and took down a sawn-off messenger gun. He broke it open and checked to see that it was loaded. When he saw the two gaping holes he asked, 'Where are the cartridges?'

Carter shrugged. 'I don't know. Listen, what are you doing?'

Ignoring the question, the gunfighter started to rummage through drawers, searching for a box of ammunition. He found them in a cabinet against the far wall. He took two cartridges and left the rest where they were.

'Listen, Kilraine!' Carter barked.

The gunfighter's head snapped up.

'Yeah, I know who you are. Just what do you think you're doing?'

'I came here for the scattergun. What I intend to do is go after Moore myself.'

'But that's my job. If you go after him then I'll lose the bonus.'

'You'll what?' Kilraine growled.

'For anyone who put the badge on, the mayor offered a bonus of a hundred dollars if they brought in Moore. If you do it, then I miss out.'

Kilraine was stunned. 'How many volunteered for the job?'

'Just me.'

'That's what I thought.'

Suddenly Carter had a six-gun in his right fist pointed at the gunfighter. He said, 'I can't let you go, Kilraine. That bonus is mine. I need it.'

'Maybe, kid, but you don't need to be dead.'

'What?'

'If you go out to Giles' ranch looking for Moore, they'll eat you for breakfast. They'll be burying you alongside the rest in Boothill.'

'I have to try.'

He could tell by the look in Carter's eyes that there would be no backing down from him. Kilraine sighed and said, 'All right, you go, but I'm coming with you.'

'But—'

'No buts. If we get Moore then I'll say that you did it and you can keep the bonus. But there is no way you're going out there on your own.'

Carter nodded. 'OK. But don't you want to take any more cartridges?'

'No. If I take time to reload the thing then I may as well shoot myself. Nope, the best thing to do is fire it then throw it away. Bring your six-gun into play after that. You'll understand what I'm saying if you stay alive long enough.'

'Any other words of advice?'

'Yeah, hit what you aim at and don't forget to duck.'

CHAPTER 10

When the ranch house came into view, Kilraine said, 'Let me do the talking, kid. You just listen and learn. And try not to let someone bushwhack us.'

The ranch area itself was huge. Two corrals, a large barn, large bunkhouse, a smokehouse. Giles had obviously spent quite a bit of money and done a lot of work to it after taking over. Out on the range the green pasture looked to be thick with cows and the occasional horse. When they entered the ranch yard there were only a few hands present, which was a good thing. The fewer the better.

When the two riders brought their horses to a halt, Kilraine said, 'Remember what I told you.'

Instantly the few hands who had been milling around multiplied as armed men emerged from the bunkhouse. A quick head count had them at ten. Not ideal odds. The gunfighter thumbed back the twin hammers on the shotgun as it lay cradled across his lap.

Kilraine said at the top of his voice so all could

hear, 'We're here for Moore.'

They just stared at him.

There was movement on the porch of the ranch house as the door swung open and two men emerged. One was Moore, the other Kilraine had never seen before but was certain that this was Giles.

'What are you doing on my land, Kilraine?' the rancher snapped.

'We've come after Moore for the murder of Winters.'

'Under whose authority?' Giles sneered.

'The sheriff, here.'

The rancher glared at Carter. 'There's no sheriff in Bowen unless I say so.'

'I guess the mayor forgot to mention that when he appointed me,' Carter shot back. Kilraine had to give it to the kid. Once he committed to something, he saw it through.

'Watch your lip, boy,' Moore snarled.

'Are you going to come quietly, Moore?' Carter asked.

Damn kid.

'Who said I shot him?'

'He did. He's still alive,' the new sheriff said, leaving out the grim possibility that Winters wasn't likely to see out the day.

'Not with three bullets in him he ain't,' Moore snorted.

'So, you're admitting you shot him?' the gunfighter asked.

'What if I am?'

'Then I'm taking you in,' Carter said, drawing a line in the sand.

Kilraine shook his head and watched Moore come down the steps and walk out into the yard. The foreman dropped his hand to his six-gun and said, 'Make your play, punk. I ain't going with you.'

Out of the corner of his eye, the gunfighter saw one of the hands start to bring his Winchester carbine up. Kilraine moved the messenger gun slightly and depressed one of the twin triggers.

The hammer fell and the weapon bucked and roared, causing the horse beneath him to lurch forward a step. The charge of buckshot caught the would-be killer flush and thrust him back with a violent shove.

Kilraine swung the shotgun back to cover the hands next to where the dead man had stood, while he drew his Colt. It snapped into line and barked savagely. Another armed hand went down, this time with a .45 slug in his chest.

'*Stop*!' Giles shouted above the rolling echo of the shots.

Beside Kilraine, Carter was stunned by the sudden violence of it all. His hand rested on his gun butt, lacking the strength to draw it. With the Messenger gun still pointed at a group of cowhands and the Colt now shifted and pointed at Giles, they had reached a stalemate.

'You got something to say?' the gunfighter asked.

'Yes, stop killing my men.'

'They started it.'

'No, you did by coming here.'

'With good reason. Now are you going to hand Moore over?'

Giles shook his head. 'No. You'll have to take him. And somehow I don't think you'll be able.'

Kilraine looked around the yard. There were still eight armed men there plus Moore and Giles. He could threaten to shoot the rancher if he didn't hand Moore over but somehow, he didn't think the man would bluff so easily. Probably best to live and fight another day. But at least now they knew he wouldn't be trifled with. The gunfighter nodded. 'You could say that. All right, we'll leave.'

'Wait, Kilraine,' Carter started to protest.

'We're leaving, kid. Live to fight another day.'

'What if I don't want you to leave?' Moore sneered.

The gunfighter said, 'Tell him to back down, Giles. I will kill him.'

'Kel, leave it. There'll be another time.'

Moore didn't like it, but he did as asked. 'All right. But this ain't over.'

The two riders turned their horses and rode out of the yard. As they left, Giles said to Moore, 'Have someone follow them. Make sure they leave.'

'Why did you let them run us off like that?' Carter snapped. 'We showed them a yellow streak a mile wide.'

'We made our point and showed common sense,' Kilraine pointed out. 'Besides, I've seen our friend

Giles before. I can't quite remember when, but I'm sure it was over Kansas way.'

'You know him?'

'Didn't say that. Said I'd seen him.'

'So, what are we going to do now?'

'See if he sends someone to follow us. He's up to something and I want to know what it is.'

They rode further along the trail until they reached a large outcrop of rocks. Kilraine eased his horse off the trail and Carter followed him. They dismounted and then waited. Five minutes later the rider appeared. The gunfighter waited until he'd ridden past and then stepped out, six-gun in hand, and said, 'Just hold it there.'

The cowhand eased his horse to a stop and sat there waiting for his accoster to speak. 'Get him down, Carter.'

'Yes, sir.'

The new sheriff hurried across to the rider and almost dragged him from the saddle. He relieved him of his six-gun and then walked him back towards the rocks, where Kilraine waited patiently.

'What are you up to?' the gunfighter asked.

'Making sure you leave.'

'What's your name?'

'Penrose.'

'That was easy, wasn't it?' Kilraine commented. 'Now for the trickier ones. What's your boss up to?'

'What do you mean?'

'Your boss wants all of the valley and he's pushing folks off by any means he thinks necessary. Why?'

'I don't know.'

Kilraine drew his Colt and cocked the hammer. He then placed it under the hand's chin. 'Let's try again.'

'What's he up to, Penrose?'

'He's bringing in more cows.'

'How many?'

'Five thousand.'

'When?'

'A few days.'

'Where from?'

'Kansas. A trail crew is bringing them in. That's why he wants the valley.'

'Fine, get out of here,' Kilraine said and watched Penrose quickly mount and ride towards the ranch.

'Now we know why he wants the ranches,' the gunfighter said.

'There is one problem, though,' Carter pointed out.

'What's that?'

'He doesn't have your ranch, or the Circle B, and he'll need at least one of them to support the extra cows. And soon.'

'Do you know Bentley?'

'Yeah, do you?'

'I know him to look at from the last time I was here. How many hands does he have?'

'Five or so plus two sons.'

'Get over there and warn him. I'd say Giles will try him tonight or the next. He needs to be ready.'

'OK. What are you going to do?'

'I'm headed back to town. There's a couple of things I want to see about.'

'OK. I'll get over there now.'

'Good. Watch yourself. Just warn Bentley and then get back to town.'

CHAPTER 11

Paul Bentley saw the rider coming in across the flat and paused from saddling his piebald. He squinted his aging eyes and called over to his eldest son, 'Rick, who's that coming across the flat? My eyes are playing up on me and I can't blamed see.'

Rick came out of the stables, a pitchfork in his hands, and turned to look at the rider. He raised his right hand to shield them from the sun's glare and said, 'It's Eli Carter, Pa.'

'Now what in tarnation do you suppose he wants out here?' Bentley muttered.

'No idea, Pa, but we're about to find out.'

'Huh? Oh.'

Carter brought his mount to a halt in the yard and climbed down from the saddle. He touched his hat brim and said, 'Howdy, Mister Bentley, Rick.'

Bentley saw the badge pinned to Carter's chest. He frowned and asked in a gruff voice, 'What fool would pin that thing on you?'

Carter looked down and then back up. 'The mayor.'

'Always said the man wasn't right in the head. What brings you out here, *Sheriff* Carter?'

'Kilraine thinks Giles will make a play for your ranch tonight or tomorrow. Said to come out and warn you.'

'Kilraine, you say?'

'Yes, sir.'

The rancher's brown eyes narrowed. 'If you're the sheriff, how come he's the one giving orders?'

'We were just over at Giles' spread. . . .'

'You and him? Why?'

'We went there to arrest Moore for the murder of Cal Winters.'

Gray eyebrows raised. 'Winters is dead?'

Carter nodded. 'Yes, sir. We went there to arrest him—'

'You and Kilraine? What was Kilraine doing out there with you?'

'He wouldn't let me go on my own,' Carter explained.

'At least someone showed sense.'

'Will you just shut your yap and listen?' Carter snapped.

The rancher's eyes sparked. 'Speak, boy.'

'Kilraine sent me out here to warn you about Giles. He's got a herd coming in and he'll either want to put it here or the Jefferson place. Kilraine figures it'll be here so you need to get ready.'

'Are you sure?' Rick asked Carter.

'No. But if he has five thousand head coming in, then like I said, he needs to put them somewhere.'

Bentley studied him and nodded. 'OK, let's assume you're right. You're the sheriff, what do you intend to do about it?'

Carter's mind raced. He'd never really thought that far ahead. After a moment the rancher grew impatient. 'Well? What do you intend to do?'

Carter's face took on a determined expression and he climbed down from the saddle, taking his Winchester with him. 'I'm going to fight with you.'

Bentley's weathered face brightened, and his mouth turned up at the corners. 'Hell, son. You might just be good enough to wear that badge yet.'

'Hey, Pa, what are you doing?'

Kilraine turned away from tying his horse to the hitch rail and gave Lucy a warm smile. 'Hey yourself. Does your ma know where you're at?'

Lucy nodded. 'Yes.'

The gunfighter gave her a questioning look and she stared at the ground. 'Lucy?'

'Maybe not,' she said meekly.

Sighing, Kilraine said, 'Come on, I'll take you back to Homer's.'

'Can't I stay with you?'

'Not now, Squirt.'

'Hey, I'm not a squirt. I'm a big girl.'

'Yes, you are. But things are happening at the moment and it's safer for you to stay with your ma, OK?'

'OK.'

He scooped her up in his arms and she gave a squeal of delight. Then Kilraine put her atop his horse and untied it from the hitch rail. 'Where are we going?' she cried out.

'I'm taking you home.'

The gunfighter started to lead the horse and his daughter along the street when he saw the rider coming towards them. There was something about the way he carried himself that drew Kilraine's attention.

As he drew closer, Kilraine recognized him. Utah Williams. As they passed, Williams nodded at the gunfighter and a cold chill ran down his spine. It looked as though Giles had just upped the ante.

After Williams had gone past, Kilraine reached up and took Lucy down amid howls of protests. She stood in the middle of the main street staring up at her father and her pleas were suddenly stopped by the look in his eyes, which scared her.

'Go back to your mother, Lucy. Now.'

She ran off and never looked back.

It was a little past nine in the evening when Kilraine walked into Bowen's second saloon, the Whiskey Rose. He knew Williams was there because he'd seen the gunfighter go in.

The bar was noisy and filled with cigarette smoke. He saw a whore standing on the stairs, a cowboy's arm around her shoulder as they both looked out across the room. Kilraine walked up to the bar and ordered a drink. The fat-faced barkeep brought him a beer in a tall mug with a handle, froth running down its sides. He placed it on the counter and took the gunfighter's money.

Kilraine sipped his beer and looked into the large mirror behind the bar. He used it to run a cautious eye over the room until he found what he wanted. Then he turned and walked towards the table where Utah Williams sat playing cards with two other men.

'Mind if I sit in?' he asked, his eyes focused on Williams.

The man to his right said, 'Sure, Kilraine, take a seat.'

'Mind if I sit in, Utah?'

'I don't mind, Kilraine.'

The second man said, 'Say, you fellers know each other?'

'Not professionally,' Williams said.

'Not yet, anyway,' Kilraine added.

The gunfighter pulled out the vacant chair and sat down. The man on his left, whose name was Morris, dealt out five cards each. Kilraine drew a pair of twos. He threw away three cards and took three from the dealer and his hand remained the same. As soon as the betting began, he threw his hand away.

After four hands, Kilraine's money pile remained roughly the same. His fifth saw him sitting on a full house, jacks and tens. He looked across the table at Williams and asked, 'You just passing through, Utah?'

Williams stared at him and said, 'After I conduct a

little business.'

The two other players seemed to freeze what they were doing and eyed Williams cautiously.

'Someone I know?' Kilraine asked.

Williams nodded. 'I think so. Maybe even well.'

'How much?'

'A thousand.'

'Must be a mighty dangerous man.'

'Depends, I guess.'

The other two men edged their chairs back and rose to their feet. Kilraine never took his eyes from the man across the table. 'When are we going to do this?'

'When would you like?'

The gunfighter was suddenly aware that the saloon had gone quiet and all eyes were concentrated on them. 'Bit crowded in here. Wouldn't want anyone to catch a stray bullet.'

'Too dark outside. Wouldn't want anyone to think I had an unfair advantage when I kill you.'

'How about we do it in the morning then? Just after sunup? Should be nice and clear about then.'

Williams nodded. 'Why not?'

Kilraine climbed to his feet. 'I'll see you then.'

CHAPTER 12

'They're coming,' Rick Bentley whispered harshly out of the darkness. From where he was hidden in the barn's loft he could see the pinpricks of flaming torches bobbing up and down with the movement of the horses.

'What the hell are you whispering for, boy?' his father snapped. 'It ain't like they can blame well hear you.'

'I said they're coming, Pa!'

'Dad blast it, there ain't no need to shout, I heard you the first time,' Bentley growled.

Carter shook his head and levered a round into the breech of the Winchester. He said, 'Are you two done jabbering?'

'Who are you talking to, boy?'

'You, old man. Unless you want to lose this fight, I suggest you get ready.'

'Damn young whipper-snapper,' Bentley grumbled. 'Are the rest of you all ready?'

'Sure boss.'

'Yeah, Pa,' the other Bentley son called from near the bunkhouse.

'Don't shoot until I do,' Carter told them. 'If you do, you'll blow it before it begins.'

They all melted back into the shadows and waited, rifles cocked and ready to fire. The low rumble of hoofbeats reached out across the landscape as the riders approached, their staccato drum seemed to vibrate in the night air. Carter gripped the Winchester tightly, nerves coursing through his body, doubts filling his mind. Part of him wished that Kilraine was here with them.

The drumming grew steadily louder, the glow from the torches larger as they drew closer. Then Carter could make out the figures, rising and falling in their saddles. Soon they were close enough that he could count them by the torches they held. Ten of them. Come to do the devil's work this night.

They dragged their mounts to a halt in the yard, horses stamping and snorting. Carter could hear Moore's voice starting to issue orders to the night riders. One of them broke away from the milling group and made to throw his burning brand up onto the roof of the ranch house.

The action snapped Carter out of his trance and the Winchester came up to his shoulder. He snapped off a shot, flame belching from the muzzle of the carbine, and the bullet hammered into the rider from the side. The torch fell short and the man slumped in his saddle before falling to the ground at the horse's feet.

Suddenly the rest of the Circle B crew opened fire and soon saddles began to empty with regular monotony. Shouts of pain could be heard above the gunfire along with the shriek of a wounded horse from the inevitable stray slug.

One of Giles' killers swung his horse about amid the chaos and pointed it back the way he'd come. It lurched forward and started to break into a ground-eating canter. Carter came around from his cover and fired after him. The rider threw up his arms and parted company with the fleeing mount.

Then came the cries of 'Don't shoot! We give up! We've had enough!'

The firing died away and of the ten who'd ridden into the Circle B ranch yard, only three remained in the saddle. It had been swift, bloody and violent.

Carter moved forward with the rest of the circle B men and they surrounded the remnants of the group of would-be killers. One of them was Jimmy.

'You dirty sons of bitches, you killed Ed!' he exclaimed. 'You killed my friend.'

'You bastards shouldn't have tried to burn my place down then, should you?' Bentley growled. 'You got what you deserved.'

'You go to hell,' Jimmy cursed.

'Hey, over here,' one of the hands called out. 'It's Moore. He's deader than a bee in a blizzard.'

Carter felt a surge of relief flow through him and then guilt as everything that had happened began to sink in.

'I guess he won't be killing any more people

around these parts,' Bentley growled.

'What's the tally?' Carter asked.

'There's five dead, two wounded, and these three.'

'Mr Bentley, have you got a wagon to transport all of these men back to town, the dead included?'

'I guess so.'

'Thank you.'

'No, son, thank you. If it weren't for you, then we would have been none the wiser about this attack and would have lost it all. Maybe I would have lost one of my boys even. Since their ma died, they're all I have.'

'Well, it wasn't exactly all me. Kilraine had a lot to do with it.'

'You were here. But when I see him, I'll be sure to mention something. Anyhow, let's do something with these corpses before they start stinking up the place. You can take them into Bowen in the morning.'

'You don't have to do this,' Grace said.

Kilraine shook his head, confused. 'I don't understand you, woman. One minute you don't want me doing something, then you do, and all of a sudden you don't. But you know how I feel about it so make up your mind.'

She watched him buckle on his Colt and tie the rawhide thong to his thigh. He straightened up and adjusted the weapon in its holster. Then Grace watched him check the loads. All the things she

110

remembered him doing from all those years ago. It was a ritual to him that came as second nature.

When he'd finished, Grace moved forward into his arms and kissed him on the lips. 'You'd better come back to us, Jared Kilraine.'

'I'll do my best.'

He turned away and left Grace in the doctor's living room. He walked outside, through the gate, and turned right, walking along the street. Already a large crowd had begun to gather with the expectation of seeing something special this day.

When he reached the saloon, Kilraine stopped. He saw Williams waiting patiently, seated on a chair outside the doors. 'Was beginning to think you weren't coming.'

'Wouldn't miss it.'

Williams climbed to his feet and started down the steps onto the street past Kilraine. They separated and put some twenty feet between themselves. On the boardwalk behind and to the left of Kilraine, there was movement and Grace pushed between two men who were standing there, waiting to observe the goings on.

The gunfighter never noticed, however, and flipped the leather hammer thong off the Peacemaker's hammer. Then he left his hand poised there next to the gun butt. Both men stood facing each other like gladiators of their chosen profession.

The expectant crowd held their collective breath in anticipation of the showdown as the two men stood there. Tension built, palpable, almost tangible, probably able to be cut with a knife. And then the hushed silence was shattered by the crash of a six-gun.

Kilraine crashed to the hard-packed street as a deep, burning pain washed through his body from back to front. Grace cried out and ran forward. She dropped at her husband's side, frantically fussing over the fallen man.

Utah Williams, six-gun half drawn, stared down at the sight before him. Anger coursed through his veins at being cheated by a coward. A shout from the crowd went up and a cowboy stepped forward. It was Best. 'Got the son of a bitch!'

Glaring eyes burned holes into the rejoicing cowhand and Williams cursed him. 'You cowardly son of a bitch. What did you do?'

'I killed him is what I did. I did your job for you.'

Williams' anger boiled over, and his Colt leaped into his hand. Another shot rocked the main street and the back-shooter fell forward, a slug in his chest.

Grace lifted her head and shouted, 'Someone get the doctor! He's still alive!'

Carter rode along the main street of Bowen beside the wagon that Rick Bentley drove. In the back were five dead men, stiff and cold. Beside them were their two wounded compatriots. The three who'd escaped the gun battle unscathed were tied on horses being led by the young sheriff.

As they travelled along, Mayor Hannigan suddenly appeared and blocked their path. 'Where the hell have you been, Carter? While you were off galli-vanting around the countryside all hell was breaking loose in town. Gunfights in the street.'

The young sheriff cast a thumb back over his shoulder. 'I was a little busy with this lot, Mayor.'

For the first time, the rotund mayor began to take in the rest of the macabre caravan. 'Who are these people?'

'Giles' men. They hit the Circle B last night. Only we were waiting for them.'

'Damned murder is what it was,' snarled Jimmy.

'Shut up, Jimmy,' Carter snapped. 'What's this about a gunfight?'

'You did all this to Giles' men?'

'Yes, now —'

'Oh, he's not going to like this,' the mayor said, his face paling noticeably.

'Damn it, Hannigan, tell me about the damn gun-fight.'

Hannigan gave Carter an indignant look. 'I beg your pardon. I'll—'

'Shit, will you tell me already?'

'OK, OK. It was Kilraine and Utah Williams.'

Carter's pulse quickened. 'What happened?'

'One of Giles' men shot Kilraine in the back is what happened. Then Williams shot him for doing it.'

'Is he alive?'

'Kilraine?'

'Yeah.'

'He was when they took him to Doc Jackson's.'

Carter started his horse forward. 'Come on, Rick, let's get this lot done. I want to check on Kilraine.'

Hannigan had to step aside or risk getting run down. He muttered something to himself and then called after them. 'What about Moore?'

'He's dead.'

CHAPTER 13

The glass shattered against the stone fireplace with a resounding crunch. Giles whirled on Utah Williams and snarled, 'Why didn't you kill him instead of my man? Christ, it's what I'm paying you for.'

'If he lives then I'll kill him. If he doesn't then I want my money.'

'What? You didn't even shoot him.'

'I would have if your man hadn't interfered. The way I see it, that's on you.'

'The hell you say.'

Williams just stared at the rancher, unmoved. Finally, Giles said, 'Fine, if you want that money, then you can earn it. The new sheriff cost me good men, I want you to get them out of jail and put a bullet in the young punk's hide.'

'That'll be an extra thousand.'

Giles waved him away with a flick of his hand. 'Fine. Just don't mess it up.'

'Just keep your men out of the way.'

'I want you to run the bastard Bentleys off their place. Today.'

'I may need a few extra men for that.'

'OK. No problem. The herd is due in at some time. Meet it and have Roach push the cattle straight onto it. After he's done that, take him and his crew with you. Don't leave any of the Bentleys alive. I want no more problems from them.'

'Hey, Doc, how's he doing?'

Jackson stepped out through his front door and onto his stoop. He shook his head. 'He's not good, Eli. I got the bullet out, but he's lost a lot of blood.'

'Is he going to die?'

'It's hard to say,' he acknowledged. Then he nodded towards the star pinned to the young sheriff's chest. 'When they told me you'd taken that thing on I didn't want to believe it. I guess it's true.'

'If you've got a minute there's a couple of fellers over at the jail who might need you to patch them up. Couple of Giles' men.'

Jackson gave him a questioning look and Carter filled him in on the previous night's events.

'Good Lord, Eli. You need to lay low. Giles isn't going to like this one bit.'

'Neither is he going to like the fact that Kilraine is still alive. Can he be moved?'

'Hell no! Not if you don't want to kill him.'

'Something tells me we may have no choice, Doc. I'll be back after to check.'

Carter turned and walked away. Watching him go,

Jackson couldn't help but notice that the boy of the day before was now suddenly a man.

Callum Roach sat astride his buckskin and watched as his men pushed the five thousand-strong herd onto the Circle B range. Beside him, on his own horse sat Utah Williams. The big trail boss hunched his shoulders and adjusted his position in the saddle. 'How far you want us to push them?'

Williams shrugged. 'This should do. They'll spread out as they feed. We'll go and pay the owner a visit now.'

'I'll gather the boys.'

Apart from being big, Roach was hard and unforgiving. He was also a killer. Men from Texas to Kansas had died under his guns. What were a few more here in Montana?

Rick Bentley thundered into the yard on a tall bay and came clear of the saddle before the animal had even stopped. He'd no sooner hit the ground when he started shouting, 'Pa! Pa!'

Bentley emerged from the house and growled, 'You'd better have a good excuse boy for riding that horse in here like that or you'll be for it.'

'Someone's moved a large herd of cows onto our east range. Now they're riding this way.'

'Damn it. I knew Kilraine getting shot would lead to trouble. Get into town, son. Find Carter and tell him what's happening. We'll try to hold whoever it is until you get back.'

Suddenly riders topped the ridge east of the ranch house. One of the hands called out and Bentley looked up and saw them. He whirled and snapped. 'Don't just stand there boy, get gone.'

'Yes, Pa,' Rick replied and ran for his lathered horse.

Bentley watched his son gallop away and a sobering thought crossed his mind as he wondered whether he'd ever see the boy again.

The riders swept down off the ridge towards the ranch, and hands scattered to take up position and meet the charge. They started firing when the riders were still two hundred yards out.

'God damn it!' Bentley roared. 'Who told you all to start firing?'

The shouting did him no good for the shooting drowned out his voice. Instead he brought up his own weapon and joined in.

By the time the riders thundered into the ranch yard the defenders had only emptied two saddles. Meanwhile, the experience of the drovers shone through with accurate fire. The hands of the Circle B were whittled down at a steady rate. Suddenly Bentley saw his second son fall. He cried out, and without thinking, the old man came to his feet from behind a water trough.

Two bullets plowed into his chest and he fell to the hard-packed earth. As the light began to fade in his eyes as the darkness closed in, he looked up at a face that floated before his eyes. It was one he'd never seen before. With blood sliding from the corner of his mouth and his voice thick with the liquid he managed to say, 'You'll get yours, you son of a bitch.'

Williams looked up from where Bentley lay and called across to Roach, 'Burn it. All of it.'

Rick Bentley found Carter at the jail. He burst into the office and said, 'You gotta come quick. The ranch is under attack. They've pushed cows onto our range.'

Carter came up from his seat and said, 'Head over to the saloon while I get my horse. See if there is anyone willing to help us.'

By the time Carter had saddled his horse and gone to the saloon, he found Rick outside on his own. 'What happened?'

'The bastards are all cowards. Not one of them would help.'

'We'll see,' Carter said, a determined expression on his face. He stomped up the steps and across the boardwalk. When the doors to the Western Pines Saloon opened and he walked in, everything went quiet.

'I'm looking for some people to form a posse. The Circle B is in trouble and they need our help. Who's with me?'

No one moved.

'None of you?'

'Looks that way, don't it, boy?'

The voice belonged to Mills from Giles' spread. 'Why don't you just go away and leave things that don't concern you be?' he said with a sneer.

'Can't do that,' Carter said firmly. 'Won't do it.'

Mills took a couple of steps forward. 'Then I'll just have to make you.'

Carter let his hand dangle close to his gun butt. He licked his lips nervously and waited for Giles' killer to make his move. The crowd was hushed with the anticipation of the first major test of the young sheriff's gun skill.

Mills gave him a cold smile and said, 'Last chance, boy. I'd take it if I was you.'

'You ain't me though, are you?'

'Suit yourself.'

Mills' gun hand moved with a fluid speed that was hard to follow with the naked eye. However, the young sheriff was well up to the task and his gun spat flame before Mills' did. The slug hammered into the killer's chest and rocked him back on his heels. Carter fired again, his second bullet spaced not far from the first. Mills fell to the ground, wounds pumping blood as his heart beat its last.

Carter punched out the empties in his six-gun and loaded fresh rounds into it. His angry gaze searched the crowd. 'So, who's coming with me?'

The crowd parted to allow Doc Jackson through. The sheriff shook his head and said, 'Not you, Doc.'

'Good lord, no. I'm not coming. I needed to tell you that Kilraine just died.'

The posse topped the ridge on the way to the Circle B and drew in hard. Before them was a group of riders coming their way. After the death of Kilraine had been announced, the posse seemed to form itself. Now Carter had ten armed riders behind him to ride to the aid of the Bentleys.

'That's Williams at the head of those riders!' Rick Bentley exclaimed. 'We're too late.'

Carter jacked a round into his Winchester and even though they were outnumbered, shouted, 'At them, boys!'

The townspeople rode forward hard into the throng of the hands. Weapons thundered as the violent struggle ripped the day apart. Somewhere amongst it all, Rick Bentley fell with a bullet in his chest. Roach took a bullet to the throat that ended his trail drive days. Others fell under the ferocity of the fight until the two groups split apart, not wanting any more to do with the killing.

Of the townsfolk Carter took with him, only four remained in their saddles. On the other side, Utah Williams and five trail hands remained. It had been so brutal that for years to come, people would talk about it as the first battle in which the town of Bowen started to fight back.

A wagon came out a few hours later to collect the dead.

CHAPTER 14

Two days later, it was raining when they buried the gunfighter. People stood there in the wet, heads bowed as the preacher droned on about how Kilraine had led a violent life but had always fought for the side of good. It was a somber affair, made even more so by the sight of the gathered, rain pouring off their clothes.

Someone had rigged a canvas between four posts and beneath it stood Grace and Lucy Jefferson. The little girl dug at the mud with her shoe as she waited patiently for the priest to finish. Once he was done, the crowd dispersed, leaving a lone figure standing there.

Carter's anger had been building since the fight and news of the gunfighter's death. He'd been seriously contemplating what he could do to stop Giles and his megalomaniacal quest for power. The law was useless to him. Although he tried to uphold it, Giles had more men, more guns, and was willing to do anything necessary to achieve his goal.

Men had already moved onto the Jefferson land and the cattle were on the Circle B from the other day. He assumed that it wouldn't be long before they came for him. He was the final obstacle still with any fight left in him.

Well if that's what they wanted, then he'd give them a fight that they'd remember for a long time to come. Carter reached up and ripped the star free of his shirt. He looked down into the hole and said, 'I'm sorry, Kilraine, but there's only one way this can be done.'

Then he tossed the badge onto the lid of the coffin and turned away.

Carter walked along the boardwalk, large droplets of water dripping from his jacket as he went. Once he reached the jail he entered to find that the cells were empty. Someone had set the prisoners free. His eyes darted about the room as though searching for a hidden assailant. Carter shrugged. 'What the hell.'

He walked over to the gun rack and took down the messenger gun, two Winchesters, and then crossed to get his saddle-bags. He filled them with spare ammunition and threw them over his shoulder. Scooping the weapons up from the desk, he turned to leave and found Grace standing in the doorway.

'What are you doing, Eli?' she asked him.

She was still dressed in black and it made him feel uncomfortable. 'I figure it's only a matter of time before they come after me, Grace. So, I'm not going to sit around until they decide it's time. If I'm going

123

to go out, it'll be on my terms.'

'Don't do anything silly, Eli. Jared wouldn't like it. He had faith in you.'

'Thank you for the kind words, but this fight ain't of my choosing. Giles and his people have killed a lot of good folks. They've moved onto the circle B as well as your pa's place again.'

'Oh, Eli. I wish you would reconsider.'

'The only way to reconsider is to put my tail between my legs and run like a rabbit. And I ain't about to do that.'

He walked towards the doorway where she stood. Leaning down, he kissed her on the cheek and said, 'Look after that little girl of yours, Grace.'

It was still raining when Carter stepped out onto the boardwalk. The afternoon was gloomy, made more so by the lack of sunshine. He glanced to his left and saw the figure walking along the street though the thickening muck.

Carter's blood ran cold. 'Grace, come out here.'

She emerged from within the jail and asked, 'What is it?'

'Go back to the doc's place.'

'What's wrong?'

Carter didn't look at her. He just watched the man approach through the curtain of rain. When Grace saw the figure she asked, 'Who is it?'

'I don't know. Just go.'

Grace hesitated.

'Go!' Carter snapped.

She hurried off, leaving him standing there. He

watched the figure stop and bring its hand up. Then came the flat report of a six-gun firing and the bullet gouged splinters from the awning post close to Carter's head.

He dropped the weapons save for one of the Winchesters, then raised that to his shoulder and snapped off a shot. The shooter ducked to his left and up onto the boardwalk, looking for cover. Carter worked the lever and fired the Winchester with practised ease, not letting up until the magazine on the Winchester ran dry. After which, Carter discarded it and picked up the other one.

Another slug whipped past Carter's head as he went to work with the second carbine. A continuous roll of thunder rocked the main street and when the last shot was fired, Carter backed up and disappeared down the alley. He needed a horse and he needed to get the hell out of town.

Late the following afternoon, as purple and red fingers reached out across the sky and the sun was all but hidden behind the distant mountains, Carter sat atop a ridge overlooking the Circle B range. Below him, smoke rose from a campfire where six men sat eating supper.

He slid from the saddle and drew the carbine from his saddle boot. He levered a round into the breech and sighted along the barrel. He squeezed the trigger and watched the cowboys around the fire scatter. It was the only warning shot he'd give them. One of them picked up his rifle and started to search the ridge for the origin of the shot. Carter's Winchester cracked again and this time it was the cowboy who went down.

Shifting his aim, Carter fired again, wounding a second cowhand. He jacked in another round and fired at a third man. Another hit. Then he stopped and watched them scatter.

After they had gone and the darkness settled in, Carter rode down to the fire. One of the hands was still alive. The bullet had hit him down low in the abdomen. He looked up and saw Carter. 'You.'

He nodded. 'Yeah, me.'

'You shot at us from ambush.'

'I gave you the same chance you gave the others that you men have been killing.'

'What now. You just shoot me?'

Carter shook his head. 'If you can get on your horse, you'll have a chance. And if you see Giles, tell him this is only the beginning.'

Giles glared at the gunfighter and growled, 'You were meant to take care of this the other day. And now that young upstart is riding around killing my men.'

'What can I say? He's hard to find.'

'What is it you need? More money? More men? You heard what he said. This is only just beginning.'

Suddenly the window exploded inwards, the sound of distant shots rolling through the night air. Giles and Williams dropped to the floor of the study. More bullets followed, one shattering the lamp on

Giles' desk. The oil from it spilled across the dark timber and the flame ignited it.

Hungry orange flames licked at the life-giving liquid and spread, taking on a life of their own.

Williams crossed to the shattered window, his boots crunching the glass beneath them. He pulled back one of the curtains and peered around the window frame. Outside came the sound of the hands stirring and leaving the bunkhouse.

The shooter fired again from his hide, and the gunfighter thought he saw a muzzle flash and fired back.

'Did you get him?' Giles called out.

Williams shook his head. 'I doubt it.'

But no more shots came. Whoever had been out there was now gone.

Coming to his feet, Giles snarled, 'It was him. It had to be him. Get out there and find the bastard, now.'

'You might want to put that fire out,' Williams said.

'Christ, he's trying to burn my place down. Don't just stand there, do something.'

Men burst into the room and saw the flames growing larger. Almost comically they started to try to extinguish the fire. But before long the flames had taken over the room, and then the house. Giles' kingdom was going up in smoke, and beginning to crumble.

From where he sat atop his horse, Carter watched

the ranch house burn, the orange glow lighting the immediate vicinity like a giant bonfire. It hadn't been part of his plan, and he hadn't meant for it to burn, but hell, who cared? Giles was only getting what he deserved.

Men scurried about like ants as they tried to extinguish the flames in a losing battle. Eventually they just stood back and watched it burn.

The sound of hoofbeats reached out through the darkness. Someone was coming, which indicated that it was time for him to leave. He turned his horse away from the scene below and urged it into a canter.

CHAPTER 15

The news of the fire spread quickly the following day, and it reached Grace Jefferson just before noon by way of Elvira Smith. 'Apparently there was a shooter and he just started firing at the house. Then somehow the house caught fire and it burned to the ground. If you ask me, it couldn't have happened to a nicer person.'

'Do they know who did it?' Grace asked.

'Word is that it was Eli.'

'Oh, no, what is he doing?'

'If you ask me, he needs to leave the territory. There's a whole posse of killers out looking for him. Some say they even have their own rope.'

'They want to hang him for that?'

'Not just that. He hit Giles' men on the Circle B. Killed some of them too. Eli is riding around like some kind of vigilante.'

A mischievous smile split the widow's lips. 'And they don't like it when they're getting some of their own back.'

'I do hope he's OK?'

'He won't be if they catch him.'

The clatter of hoofbeats drew their attention and both women stared as Giles and a handful of men rode along the main street. They eased their horses to a halt down near the Western Pines Saloon and dismounted.

A flatbed wagon approached, and the rancher snapped an order. One of his men walked out and stopped its progress. Then Giles climbed atop its bed and drew his six-gun. He fired off two shots to get some attention. Once he was sure he had it, he shouted at the top of his voice, 'My men and I are moving into town! The saloon in fact! We shall be staying there until Eli Carter is brought before me to be hung for the murder of my men! This is my town, and don't you people damned well forget it!'

He climbed down and stomped up the steps onto the boardwalk, crossed to the saloon doors and threw them open. A few moments later gunfire erupted from within, and soon after, four of Giles' men heaved the bodies of both the barkeep and the owner out onto the street.

Grace watched on in horrified silence at the cold spectacle that was unfolding before her and Elvira. The appalling situation was deteriorating quickly and seemed as though it could not get any worse. The ugly truth of the matter was that the townsfolk of Bowen were letting it happen. Not one of them had the guts to stand up and fight anymore. Not one of them was Jared Kilraine.

Carter rode into the dry arroyo lined with tall pines. On his backtrail were at least ten riders from Giles' spread, headed up by Utah Williams. They'd cut his trail not long after dawn and he'd led them into the foothills to try and shake them. But the point was fast approaching when he was going to have to turn around and try to dissuade them from following.

Ahead, a rockfall had blocked the trail and Carter had to ride up the slope and around it. On the other side of the fall, the arroyo opened out into a high-country meadow. He ground hitched the horse and climbed back up the rocks to wait.

It was twenty minutes before the first horse appeared. Williams had sent a scout on ahead of the main force, not willing to risk too many lives in the arroyo's confines. The lone rider came on and followed Carter's trail up and around the avalanche site. When the man saw the horse below, it was too late, Carter had moved in behind him and snapped, 'Hold it right there, Jimmy.'

The rider stopped and didn't move. 'Is that you, Carter?'

'Who else would it be?'

'You've really done it this time, boy. You're as good as dead when Williams catches up to you.'

'He's got to catch me yet. Get off the horse.'

Jimmy did as he was ordered, and Carter closed in behind him. He heard the crunch of boot on gravel and sneered, 'What now? You going to shoot me in the back? Not man enough to face me and do it from the front?'

'Turn around,' Carter snapped.

Jimmy did so and stared at the young man, anger glittering in his eyes. 'Come on, Eli. You reckon you're man enough?'

The butt of the Winchester arced upward and caught the cowhand under the chin. His head snapped back, and his eyes rolled back in his head. Knees buckled and Jimmy slumped to the dirt, out cold.

Carter once more made his way up to the slide and settled down behind a clump of boulders. The main bunch appeared some five minutes later, picking their way along the bottom of the arroyo. He waited patiently until he was ready and then fired. The lead rider threw up his arms and fell to the earth. Men threw themselves from the saddle and sought shelter wherever they could find it.

Bullets suddenly filled the air and began to ricochet off the rocks below Carter. He worked the lever and fired a few more times, letting them know he was still there. Then he stopped and let everything go quiet.

After ten minutes he saw the first movement from below. One of the cowhands ran from behind a tall spruce to an outcrop of rock. Carter continued to wait and the man moved again. This time, however, the young man led the man with the foresight and then squeezed the trigger. The runner dropped like a stone and never moved.

With that, the posse below opened fire and once more the rock fortress was peppered with lead. Instead of firing some more, Carter moved back down into the arroyo, collected his horse, and rode away.

A sorry-looking bunch of riders let their horses slowly make their way along Bowen's main street, heads hung low. It was three days later, and both men and mounts were exhausted.

They were met outside the saloon by Giles. 'What happened? You couldn't find him?'

'Just take a head count, Mr Giles,' Williams said scornfully. 'We found him. We buried the dead out there.'

'You let one man whip you all to a frazzle?'

Tired and saddle sore and not willing to be berated in public, Williams snapped, 'You weren't out there, were you? So you wouldn't know.'

'So get yourselves some fresh horses and get back out there.'

'These men need sleep. We'll stay in town the night and head back out tomorrow.'

Giles didn't like his orders being countermanded but he knew the gunfighter was right. 'OK, then. There's room enough here.'

'We'll just take care of our horses and be back.'

'Carver Giles, enough is enough. I demand you and your men leave town this minute.'

Giles turned to face the newcomer. Mayor Hannigan stood defiantly on the boardwalk, hands on hips. 'What you are doing is unlawful and unwanted. And we, the town, do not like it.'

'Guess what, Mr Mayor. I do not give two knobs of dog shit what you think. Now get the hell away from me.'

'I beg your pardon?' Hannigan spluttered, his face reddening.

'You heard me, you tub of lard. Get gone. I run Bowen now.'

'You do no such thing. This town is run by the town—'

The crash of a six-gun stopped Hannigan cold. His jaw dropped and his eyes bulged with shock. Grasping at his middle, his hands were drawn there by the force of the bullet smashing into him. Giles stared at him and said, 'Now maybe you'll shut up.'

The mayor fell to his knees and slumped onto his side, where he slowly bled to death gasping for air.

Looking around at the townsfolk who'd seen him shoot the mayor, Giles had a wild look in his eyes. 'If you people don't want this to happen to you, then you'll do what needs to be done. I want that son of a bitch, Carter.'

Carter walked out of the darkness and said, 'You bastards don't belong here. Give me one reason why I shouldn't just shoot you dead right now.'

'We ain't done nothing,' one of the hands blurted out. 'We're just watching the cows.'

'Stand up, all of you.'

Each of the six men came to their feet. 'Get your clothes off. All of them.'

The hands slowly began discarding their clothes under Carter's watchful eye as well as that of his Winchester. Once they were done, the young man indicated to one of them, saying, 'Go and saddle all the horses. Then bring them into the firelight. The rest of you put your clothes on the fire.'

'The hell I will,' one of the men growled.

The carbine whiplashed and the slug hammered into the ground between the cowboy's bare feet. He jumped and cursed at Carter, to which the young man replied, 'Put them on the fire.'

The flames soon leaped high into the air, hungrily feeding on the natural fibers of the cloth. With that done the other cowboy emerged leading the horses. 'Now hook the six-guns over the saddle-horns.'

The naked cowboy followed the instructions and stepped back from the horses.

'All right,' Carter said. 'Start walking.'

'Where? Where are we going to go? We've got no clothes.'

'I don't really care. You don't need clothes to walk. Now move.'

Amid grumbling and curses, the six cowboys turned and began to walk.

The following morning when they arrived in Bowen, all they could do was hide their nakedness with pieces of brush they'd picked up along the trail. They were soon the laughing stock for the people in town. All Carter had achieved was to make his enemies even angrier, and Giles even more determined to rid himself of the young avenger.

CHAPTER 16

When the odd pair arrived in town, they turned heads. One was a bear of a man dressed in buckskins. The other was a dog. A massive dog half the size of a small horse. Nobody had ever seen anything like it before. The man, however, was named Wilhelm Schultz, or The German, a manhunter of great reputation. The dog he'd raised from a pup. It was a German boarhound.

They stopped outside the saloon and the big man climbed down from his horse. He brushed down his stinking buckskins and climbed the steps. The dog followed him up to the doors and then lay down to one side, keeping the entrance clear. There were no words from the manhunter, the boarhound just knew what was expected of him.

Schultz stopped inside the door and spoke in a loud, heavily accented voice. 'I'm looking for Giles.'

Giles looked up from the table and stared at the stranger. 'You the manhunter I sent for? The German?'

Schultz nodded and gave a grunt. 'I am.'

'You made good time. Three days.'

'I wasn't busy.'

'You bring your dog?'

'Uh huh. You give me money.'

Giles shook his head. 'You ain't gone and found him yet.'

'Half the money first.'

'Nope.'

'Goodbye.'

Schultz turned and started to walk out the door. Behind him an anxious look crossed Giles' face and he called after the German, 'All right. We'll do it your way.'

The manhunter turned around. 'Thousand now, another thousand when it's done.'

'OK, I can do that.'

'Good,' the manhunter said and started to leave once again.

'Hey, where are you going?'

'To find the boy you want me to kill.'

'I don't want him dead. I want him brought in alive so I can do it.'

'Dead is easier.'

'You don't even know his name.'

Schultz stopped. 'You tell me then.'

'It's Eli Carter.'

'Fine,' the manhunter grunted and kept walking.

'I have to get out there and help him.'

'Jared, no. You're dead, remember?' Grace

reminded him. 'Besides, you're not ready.'

'You saw that big guy ride by. His name is Schultz. He's a manhunter. He uses that brute of a boarhound to help bring his quarry down.'

'No, Jared. Get back into bed.'

'Doc, I need to help the kid.'

After Kilraine had been shot in the back and the bullet taken out by Jackson, the idea of killing off the legend of the gunfighter was floated. It was assumed he would be safer that way, and therefore allowed to mend. There were only two people who knew he was alive. The doctor and Grace. Not even Lucy knew her father was still alive. That had been the hardest part of the ruse. But so far, they had managed to keep the secret.

Homer Jackson shook his head. 'I'm sorry, Kilraine, but I have to agree with Grace. You ain't fit to sit a saddle yet. Maybe in a couple of days.'

'It could be too late in a couple of days.'

'That's how it is.'

'Shit!' Kilraine cursed.

'You watch your tongue, Jared,' Grace scolded. 'Before long Lucy will be saying cuss words like that.'

'Well, if she does, I sure hope she says it like she means it.'

Jackson chuckled. 'Just like you two were married all over again.'

'I can't recall her ever being this bossy,' Kilraine said.

'Bed. You can get on a horse in two days. I won't fight you then.'

'Someone still needs to warn the kid,' the gun-fighter pointed out.

Jackson said, 'I'll find someone who can do it. The only problem is, they will need to find him first.'

'Do it, Doc. And have them take him some food. He's going to need it.'

'I got some food for you too,' Crispin the gunsmith said, handing the small sack over.

'Tell the doc I said thanks,' Carter said through a mouthful of biscuit.

'You gotta be careful, Eli,' Crispin warned him. 'This manhunter is bad news. And the size of that dog he has with him, you could throw a saddle on it and ride all the way to the Mexican border.'

'I'll be fine, Cris.'

'Have you ever thought about getting out, Eli?' the gunsmith asked. 'Just point your horse in a direction and keep riding.'

'Sure. But that's not what Kilraine would've done.'

'Kilraine is dead.'

'Which makes it even more important that I stand up for the townsfolk.'

Crispin snorted derisively. 'They won't help you, Eli. Giles made sure of that when he shot the mayor.'

'He shot Hannigan?'

'Yeah. Killed him stone cold. Didn't you know?'

Carter cocked an eyebrow.

Crispin nodded. 'Yeah, right. Sorry.'

'How's Grace and Lucy doing?'

'I think they're OK.'

Carter dug into the small sack for another biscuit. 'Tell her I'm keeping an eye on her place, OK?'

'Sure. You need anything else?'

'I could do with some more ammunition.'

'I can do that. What do you need?'

'Some forty-fives and forty-five seventies. I'll fix you up when I can.'

Crispin shook his head. 'Don't worry about it. Just stay alive. I'll bring them to you in a day out at Squaw Rock.'

'OK. I'll meet you there. Thanks, Cris.'

'Stay alive, Eli.'

When Crispin mounted his horse and rode away down the slope from the tree line where Carter was camped, he wasn't aware that he was being watched. From a large outcrop of rock, the manhunter had observed his coming and going. He waited patiently to see what Carter would do before he made his move. When he sat down to eat more food, the German decided it was time to move in. He looked at his boarhound and said, 'Come.'

Climbing onto his horse, he circled around up slope so he could come down into Carter's camp from above. Once Schultz figured he'd gone far enough he dismounted and called his dog to him.

The manhunter rubbed the animal's muzzle and whispered something into its ear in German. Then with a grunt, he said, 'Hunt.'

The boarhound took off through the trees at a

gallop, a low growl deep in its throat. The German followed him downslope, a Colt Burgess lever-action rifle in his hands.

He weaved his way through the trees and around large boulders until suddenly the manhunter frowned. He stopped and listened but heard nothing. He thought the dog should have reached his quarry by now. But there was nothing. No growling, no barking, no indication of anything.

Schultz edged forward, his senses alert for anything. Then, when he came around a large outcrop of rock, he saw the boarhound sitting next to Eli Carter. The young man had his Winchester pointed at the German and said, 'You really need to feed your dog better.'

A growl rumbled in the manhunter's throat. '*Dummer verdammter hund.*'

'Drop your guns,' Carter snapped.

Schultz dropped the Colt at his feet followed by his six-gun. 'Now what?'

'You take your dog and get.'

'He's no good to me now. Maybe I shoot him.'

'Maybe you won't. Don't blame the animal, I've always had a way with them. Now, get the hell out of here. Tell Giles to come himself next time, if he's got the stones.'

'You tell him.'

'Maybe I will.'

Schultz disappeared into the trees and Carter mounted his horse. He looked down at the dog and said, 'Come on you, let's go.'

The young man rode down the slope out into the open, the dog following.

Crispin worked oil into the Winchester's mechanism and then lay it on the counter before him. He put some more oil on the rag and was about to coat the barrel when the door opened and an angry-looking Schultz entered.

The gunsmith swallowed hard when he saw the man, and tried to hide his nervousness. 'Can . . . can I help you?'

The German closed the door, locked it, and turned to face the fearful Crispin. 'I am going to ask you a few questions. You will tell me what I want to know.'

'I don't know anything,' the gunsmith blurted out.

'You will.'

'No . . . no . . . no I know nothing.'

Schultz closed the gap between them and walked around behind the counter. He reached out and grabbed the cowering man by the shirt. 'I saw you with him. Now I want to know everything.'

Although not without pain, Kilraine eased himself out of bed and into his clothes. He found his six-gun and holster in the cupboard and buckled them on. He didn't worry about the Winchester.

Outside was still dark but a wall lamp burned in the hallway for Doc Jackson. He was back and forth checking on Crispin, who'd been beaten to within

143

an inch of his life the previous day.

The gunsmith had remained conscious long enough to explain what happened to him and where he was meant to meet Carter. Now Kilraine was sneaking out before dawn to go and help him.

He started along the hallway and the door to Lucy and Grace's room opened. The gunfighter rolled his eyes thinking that he'd been discovered. Instead it was his daughter who stepped out. Her eyes widened and she was about to cry out when his hand clamped over her mouth and the gunfighter whispered, 'Don't scream, Lucy. Please don't scream.'

He eased his hand away from her mouth. 'Pa!' she blurted out in a hoarse whisper.

'Yeah, baby girl, it's me.'

The hardest thing about being dead was that his daughter slept in the next room and had been unaware that her father was still alive.

'Can you keep a secret?' he asked her.

Lucy nodded.

'Good. You can't tell anyone I'm still alive.'

'But won't they be happy like me that you are?'

'No, not everyone. OK?'

'OK. Where are you going?'

'I'm off to fight bad guys.'

She moved in close and wrapped her arms around him. 'Don't get shot again, please.'

'I'll try not to.'

'Ma is going to be cross with you, isn't she?'

He thought of Grace and nodded. 'Yeah. Now, go back to bed.'

She hugged him again and said, 'Your rifle is next to the back door.'

He ruffled her hair and said, 'Go back to bed.'

Watching her slip back into the room, he then continued toward the dining room.

CHAPTER 17

No one really remembered how the place had gained the name Squaw Rock. It wasn't even much of a rock to begin with. Apparently, it dated back to when the west was young, and the trappers roamed the land. There was plenty of water from a spring that bubbled up out of the ground, filling a small reservoir that eventually emptied into a narrow stream.

Carter had stayed there the night under a clear sky that sparkled with millions of stars. Once the ammunition arrived, he was going to raid Giles' herd, scatter it across the valley. He would try and draw some of his men out of town and then head into Bowen for a final confrontation with the son of a bitch behind it all.

Unless. . . .

The dog let out a low warning growl and came to its feet. It took a couple of steps forward and stopped. Carter dropped his hand to his six-gun and was about to take it out when a voice said, 'Leave it

146

where it is.'

Schultz emerged from the trees, a new Winchester in his grasp. The boarhound let out a louder growl and the German snorted. 'I raise him from a pup, and this is how he thanks me. Well, maybe once I kill you then he will see where he is better.'

Carter shrugged. 'Dog'll make up his own mind.'

'Maybe. Maybe he'll just come because I feed him like you.'

'You just here to kill me?'

'Yes.'

'I guess you better get it over with then.'

Carter had it in his mind that he wasn't about to let the manhunter have it all his own way. He'd throw rocks at the son of a bitch if he had to. The Winchester came up and snapped into line. Carter's hand dove for his six-gun but he knew he wasn't about to make it. The sound of a gunshot filled the morning air and the manhunter fell forward.

Carter stared in wonder at the figure standing behind the fallen giant. The one who'd just saved his life. 'Son of a bitch. Is that really you?'

Kilraine nodded. 'It's me, kid. Although I'm not sure I can call you that. You been raising hell on your lonesome like a full-growed man.'

'I don't believe it. They said you were dead.'

'Uh huh,' Kilraine acknowledged, holstering his Colt. 'There was only two people who knew I was still alive. Grace and Doc Jackson. Even Lucy thought I was dead.'

'I ain't dreaming, am I?'

'No.'

'How did you know I was here?'

The gunfighter filled him in on what had happened to Crispin and how he'd left before daylight to find Carter to help. Kilraine pointed at the dog. 'What's with the horse?'

'He likes me.'

'Really?'

'Yes. He's harmless.'

'I'll take your word for that. What were you planning on doing next?'

'I was going to try a diversion to get some of Giles' men out of town and then go after him.'

'And do what?'

'Kill him. He's just asking for it.'

'What about Williams?'

'I ain't thought that far ahead yet,' Carter allowed.

'Well, you're going to need some help,' Kilraine told him. 'I know of a way to get him so riled he won't hesitate to send his men out of town.'

'How?'

'We rob the bank. Giles keeps all his money there, so let's take it. That'll get him madder than a hornet.'

'OK. I'm in. What could be better than a bank being robbed by an ex-sheriff and a dead gunfighter?'

'Surprise!' Kilraine said smiling from beneath his pulled-down hat. For a moment he thought Burt Wells was about to faint, or die of heart failure. But

148

after a moment the color came back to his face.

'You're dead,' he gasped.

The gunfighter tilted his hat back so the other customers could see who it was. They stared in confusion, trying to work out how he had come back to life. 'Eli, tell the man why we're here.'

'In case you ain't worked it out just yet, we're going to rob your bank. That ought to make Giles happy.'

'Why don't you just take the papers to his ranch?'

'His deeds?' Kilraine asked.

'Yes, sir.'

'Get them.'

Wells hurried into his office and Kilraine turned to Carter. 'How are we looking?'

'OK, so far.'

Wells appeared with the papers in his hand. 'These are them.'

Kilraine took them and stuffed them inside his shirt. 'Why are you helping us?'

'Because Giles is crazy. He shot the mayor in cold blood and he sits over in the saloon all day drinking.'

'Well, what you can do now is go over there and tell him that we've taken the deeds to his ranch and all he has to do to get them back is meet me on the street.'

Carter's head spun around. 'Hold up, what are you doing?'

'It ends today.'

'This could end in tears, you know that?'

'I guess we'll find out. You up for it?'

149

'If I get me a chance to put a bullet in that son of a bitch, hell yeah.'

Kilraine turned back to Wells the banker. 'I guess you'd best get going then.'

Carver Giles was a far cry from the man he used to be. Living in the saloon was getting the better of him. A combination of not much sleep, copious amounts of alcohol, little food, and no personal hygiene made him look more like the town drunk than a wealthy land owner. He was in such a state that Utah Williams was ready to call it quits and pull out. They hadn't seen the German since the day before and God only knew where he was.

The saloon doors opened, and the banker Wells entered. He had a fearful expression on his face as though he was scared that he was walking into a bear's den and might never come out. When he saw that Carver Giles was actually asleep in the chair, his relief was visible.

He turned around and went to walk back out when Giles said, 'What do you want, Wells?'

The banker's face paled and Williams thought the man was going to throw up on the sawdusted floor. He opened his mouth to speak but nothing came out. Giles lifted his head and studied him. 'Well? What is it? You look like you've seen a ghost?'

'Ah . . . yes, you could say that. He was supposed to be dead. But he isn't. And now he's over in the bank.'

'Who, damn it?'

'Kilraine.'

Williams came forward in his seat. 'Are you saying that Kilraine ain't dead and that he's over there in your bank, right now?'

Wells nodded. 'Uh huh.'

'Son of a bitch.'

'That's not all.'

'No?' said Giles.

'He's got your papers for your ranch. He said if you want them back to meet him outside on the street.'

Giles eased forward and came to his feet. 'Is he on his own?'

'No, sir. Eli Carter is with him.'

The rancher picked up the half-full bottle of whiskey from the tabletop and put it to his lips. He took a long pull and placed it back on the table. 'I guess I'd best not keep the man waiting.'

Giles lurched towards the doors and out onto the boardwalk.

CHAPTER 18

The sun was bright, especially after the gloom of the saloon, and Giles raised his hand to stave off the glare. He stood on the boards for a while as he looked about. Out on the street stood Kilraine and Eli Carter. A crowd had started to gather, more in amazement that the gunfighter was still alive than anything else. Jimmy walked up beside Giles and said, 'I want part of this. I owe both these sons of bitches.'

The rancher nodded. 'Have it your way.'

Footsteps sounded on floorboards and Williams appeared in the doorway of the saloon. He ran his gaze over the street and let it linger on Kilraine. He muttered something under his breath and stepped outside. He said in a low voice, 'Kilraine is mine.'

One by one they walked out onto the street, moving with deliberate strides. An excited murmur ran through the watchers as anticipation built. Would they get their town back? Or would Giles keep his stranglehold on the town.

Out of the corner of his eye, Kilraine saw Grace and Doc Jackson appear, his wife's face etched with the fear of her husband dying. But she didn't say anything. She just had to trust that he knew what he was doing.

'You don't much look like a ghost, Kilraine,' Utah Williams said.

'Just needed time to mend.'

'And you're OK, now?'

'Good as new.'

The gunfighter nodded with satisfaction. 'Wouldn't want people to think that I took advantage of a man below his best.'

'Where are my deeds, Kilraine?' Giles snapped.

'I guess you'll have to come get them.'

Giles nodded slowly, the outward expression of his acceptance of the situation about to play out. Carter moved a few paces away from Kilraine to divide their fire. He figured that Williams would concentrate on Kilraine, so he didn't have to worry about him. Jimmy, on the other hand, was holding a personal grudge against him from the other day, so he figured him to be his main threat. By the look of Giles, he'd not be much of a problem.

And in an ideal world that's how it should have played out, violent and bloody on the main street of Bowen. But no one had counted on what happened next.

Lucy had followed her mother and Homer Jackson without their knowledge and worked her way along the crowd to where she could get a better view. When she found the right place, she was unaware of the rough-looking cowboy who'd suddenly appeared beside her. By the time she did, he'd grabbed her roughly by the arm and dragged her out onto the street.

'Mr Giles, I got us a chip here.'

'Let me go!' Lucy cried out.

'Lucy!' Grace shouted. 'Jared!'

Kilraine's blood ran cold at the sight of his daughter. 'Let her go, Giles. She's got nothing to do with this.'

The rancher's demeanor suddenly changed. 'But she does now. She is going to get me everything that I want.'

'Which is?'

Giles stared at Carter. 'Get off the street, boy.'

'I ain't going anywhere.'

'How noble. I'll put it this way. Get off the street or the girl dies.'

Carter glanced at Kilraine. The gunfighter nodded. 'It's OK.'

'But there's three of them.'

'I can count.' Kilraine said in a low voice. 'But that's my daughter, and this son of a bitch just made the biggest mistake of his life.'

The young man started for the boardwalk, but the rancher said, 'Leave your gun-belt behind. I'll not have you shooting me in the back from over there.'

With a loud curse, Carter dropped the gun-belt into the dirt at his feet and kept walking. Jimmy called after him, 'I'll see you when we're done here, Eli.'

'Is this it, Giles?' Kilraine asked. 'You three against me?'

'Seems fair to me.'

'What about you, Utah?'

'I've had enough of this place, Kilraine. I just want my money and to be shook of this town.'

'All right then. Call it.'

The three men separated and took up their positions. Without knowing it, they made the gunfighter's job easier than it possibly could have been by Williams being on his left. It meant that Kilraine could work his way along the line instead of jerking his aim back and forth.

He knew he'd have to kill Williams first. But he couldn't linger. It would have to be one shot, one kill. He needed to be at his best.

A deep breath and Kilraine's shoulder dipped. His fingers wrapped around the butt of the Colt as he started his fluid draw.

Any gunfighter worth his salt would tell you that fanning the hammer was a showman's trick that made for ridiculous, inaccurate shooting. But Kilraine wasn't a showman. He was the best in his profession.

What happened next was so unbelievably fast that no one really saw it. The noise from the gunshots seemed to roll into one and when Kilraine had finished, the three men were still upright. Dead on their feet, red blossoms on their chests.

The one who seemed stunned by it the most was Utah Williams. Never before had he seen such speed, and now never would he see it again.

He remained upright the longest and after his six-gun fell from his grasp, his legs gave out and he slumped to the ground.

Kilraine shifted his aim so the smoking barrel covered the cowboy standing with his daughter. 'Let her go.'

The stunned man did, and Lucy ran to her mother, laying her face against her. Kilraine thumbed back the hammer and said, 'Ever had one of them days where nothing seems to go your way? This is one of them.'

The Colt roared a final time and the cowboy was flung onto his back, blood flowing freely from his chest.

Kilraine holstered the gun and looked at the astonished faces of the crowd staring at him, unsure what would happen next, not wanting to miss a thing. The gunfighter turned towards his wife and daughter, then walked across and took both in his arms.

'Oh, Jared, is it finally over?'

'Yes. It's over.'

Kilraine watched a laden wagon rattle along the main street of Bowen, driven by a middle-aged man. Seated beside him was a woman of approximately the same age. Beside her were two children.

As they disappeared towards the far end of town, a voice said, 'Their name is Weston. They're taking over the Lazy G.'

The gunfighter placed the sack of flour he was holding on the flatbed wagon and turned to face the speaker. 'I see you found yourself another badge.'

Carter smiled. 'No one else wanted it. And I wasn't cut out to be mayor.'

Kilraine nodded. 'I don't know how Doc Jackson will manage that and fixing folks.'

'Just don't get sick, Jared,' Jackson said as he helped Grace carry more supplies from the store.

'Pa, look what Ma bought me.'

Lucy danced out through the doors, wearing a blue bonnet that matched her dress. Kilraine scooped her up in his arms and placed her on the wagon seat. He said, 'You look beautiful, Lucy.'

She kissed him on the cheek. 'Ma said I can have a new dress the next time we come to town since my other one is getting too small.'

He glanced at Grace and she nodded, a broad smile on her lips signifying her satisfaction at having her family back together. 'Eli, will you join us for supper this Sunday?'

He was about to answer when the boarhound appeared beside him, nuzzling his hand before sitting at his feet. He indicated the dog. 'Can I—'

'Yes, can he, Ma?'

'Only if he doesn't eat too much.'

'He's the size of a horse. How much do you think he'll eat?' the gunfighter said skeptically.

'What about you, Homer? Would you care to join us?'

'Don't mind if I do.'

'OK, then, it's all organized.'

Grace climbed up onto the seat of the wagon beside her daughter, as did Kilraine. It was then that Carter noticed something different about the gunfighter. He wasn't wearing his gun.

'Take care, Jared,' he said as Kilraine took up the reins.

'Always do, Eli,' he replied and gave the leathers a flick.

The horses lurched forward and pulled out into the middle of the street. Homer Jackson said as he watched them go, 'I hope things work out this time, Eli. Lord knows they deserve it.'

'I think it'll be fine, Doc,' Carter said.

The dog at his feet growled at an approaching rider, but they took no notice. He didn't look to be much older than Carter, with a baby face adorned with peach fuzz. But what the boarhound had noticed was the twin six-guns he wore.

He drew his mount up to the hitchrail and said, 'You two dudes ever heard of a top gun named Kilraine? Said to live around here.'

Carter and Jackson stared at him for a moment before Carter said, 'Nope. Never heard of him.'